June-tree

ALSO BY PETER BALAKIAN

Poetry
Father Fisheye (1979)
Sad Days of Light (1983)
Reply from Wilderness Island (1988)
Dyer's Thistle (1996)

Limited Editions
Declaring Generations (1981)
Invisible Estate (1984)
The Oriental Rug (1986)

Prose
Theodore Roethke's Far Fields (1989)
Black Dog of Fate (memoir, 1997)

Translation
Siamanto's *Bloody News from My Friend*
(with Nevart Yaghlian, 1996)

June-tree

New and Selected Poems

1974–2000

Peter Balakian

HarperCollins*Publishers*

HarperCollins books may be purchased for educational, business, or sales promotional use. For information please write: Special Markets Department, HarperCollins Publishers, Inc., 10 East 53rd Street, New York, NY 10022.

FIRST EDITION

Designed by Nicola Ferguson

Library of Congress Cataloging-in-Publication Data
Balakian, Peter, 1951–
June-tree : new and selected poems, 1974–2000 /
Peter Balakian.—1st ed.
p.   cm.
ISBN 0-06-019841-9
1. Armenian Americans—Poetry.   I. Title.
PS3552.A443 J8   2001
811'.54—dc21   00-047276

01 02 03 04 05   10 9 8 7 6 5 4 3 2 1

for Bruce Smith and Jack Wheatcroft

CONTENTS

FROM *REPLY FROM WILDERNESS ISLAND* (1988)

AUTHOR'S NOTE

Over the years, some of the poems from *Father Fisheye, Sad Days of Light,* and *Reply from Wilderness Island* have been revised, and titles of some poems have changed. "After We Split," "Winter Revival," "Robert Lowell Near Stockbridge," and "Post-Traumatic Shock, Newark, New Jersey, 1942" grew out of earlier poems. Grateful acknowledgment to magazines where poems in the "New Poems" section have appeared: *The Agni Review* for "Lowlands," *Ararat* for "In Armenia, 1987," *The New Republic* for "Ellis Island," *Verse* for "Jade Boat," and "The Children's Museum at Yad Vashem" in a limited edition, The Press of Appletree Alley.

I want to express my gratitude to Bruce Smith, Jack Wheatcroft, Helen, Tom Sleigh, Jay Parini, Wendy Ranan, Agha Shahid Ali, Jerry Costanzo, Stanley Moss, and to Robert Jones, Gail Winston, and Eric Simonoff. I am most grateful to Yaddo, where I have worked on many poems over the past twenty years.

—P. B.

NEW POEMS

Photosynthesis

The slips of the day-
lilies come off.

The wind blows
in from Vermont,
blows the silk kimonos

off the delphiniums,
blows the satin cowls
off the jack-in-the-pulpits.

Let it blow
the detonated-pollen
green, acid-rubbed,

plumed and rotting day—
blow into the leaves

their silver undersides
wet you at night.

Slide your tongue
into the green dark

so you can see the ultra-
violet scars on the goldfields
where the bees come in the day.

The night air rises
like steam
from a mud-pot,

and you see nothing.
Hear no voice.
See no light.

Just yourself
staring back at you
in middle age,

as if the novocain
of the sea urchin
froze your lids.

You see the window
you built

where you placed your hands
and broke your turquoise jars
and saw the stones

of scalding yellow
where the steam had burned
things back to where your private lust

and your longing for history
were colorless, and the blood
of the dianthus was gone.

You see your life rise
and slide away like steam,

feel a goat-tongue
lost in a mountain
wet you down.

The Tree

You wandered into the shade
where the mulberry leaves
were soft and etched,
where something that looked like worms
copulated in sooty black,
and the light made tracery
on the dead pond.

Because the Jews left Babylon
for a rainless place,
because men were hung in the margins.

Because Christians were booted
out of town—

the lance of a spire opens a chapter.

If you watch the letters
you'll see a flamingo twitch,
the pond's scum ruffle
like a page.

Yorkshire Dales

I came to forget the sentimental death of Vallejo,
the frozen rooms of Yerevan,
and the precious blood symbolized by the Pelican.

I came to forget the sky is dome-like and opens
(who could still believe that at my age?)

As we trip on limestone rocks,
my daughter says, "up here everything's perfect,
the world is gone."

I came to forget the limestone anyway,
and my name given to me by history.

Everywhere there was clean blue light this morning.
Everywhere cars were pumping exhaust
over the narrow stone-walled roads.

My son says, "why is there something instead of nothing?"

Past the lines of dried blood on the dale
I can see the Brontë parsonage,

I can see the faded green damask walls
and the Regency table in the dining room
where Charlotte, Emily, and Anne wrote hunched under coverlets
    and shawls.

The air fills with the sound of baby-boom melodrama

as if it rises like steam from the rocks of a hot bath

operatic, spastic, fluttering tongue

"isn't that Jackie Wilson?" my wife asks—

isn't a wing inside the heart bloodless?

Can you say *higher and higher* up here?
Are the ventricles of sound dome-blue like the sky?

for Antonia and Nigel Young

Killary Harbor

I drove through the narrow Gods—
privet and cholesterol, or
Irish creamery butter as the waiter

called it, as it shaved another day
off my life. There was no salt
and antimony, just lumpy roads

through Meath and Leitrim.
The sky was a show of flashing
mirrors as day broke on Rosses.

Tide out and weed like cow pies
on the shore. The punt down and
the EEC on the horizon,

as I read in the guidebook about pilgrims
climbing St. Patrick's barefoot
every summer.

Out of the fog a man in Wranglers and
spurred boots, clean-shaven, a cigarette
in hand, waved me down.

"Scrum-faced house at the end of the bay."
"Hop in," I said. *"You lookin'
for where John Wayne made* The Quiet Man?"

"No." *"American?"* "Yep." *"Don't look it.
You Jewish too?"* "No."
"I-talian?" "No."

The fog was lifting off the fern-scalded
mountains across the bay, and the sheep
marked red and blue looked like sweaters.

"Grace O'Malley hijacked British
ships up here, and the Choctaws
sent $500 during the famine. Not a fuckin' penny from the U.S."

We passed the rusted hulls
of fishing boats and the scaffolding
of floating mussel beds.

"The Downing Street Accord is lots of
shit; Adams' a frog on an oil slick.

When Lord Haw Haw broadcast for the Nazis
from right here, do ya think he was
a traitor or a patriot? . . . to us, I mean?"

I couldn't bring myself to tell him
I was on sabbatical and looking for
a place to write.

"They'll turn the bog to Marks & Spencer anyway."

"I'm looking for Knock-Na-Rae."

"Maeve's mountain? Two hours from
here in the other direction."

I dropped him at the scrum house
half roofless and cracked,
where the sky seemed lower than the rocks

and the hills the color
of red sheep.

for Denise and Matt Leone

In Armenia, 1987

Into a basalt cavern
I wandered, where the moon
slid like a water snake

in white skin
through the gullies
to the blond and furry wheat.

A grubby man,
I dug toward the damp smell
of a water channel—

and found a shard
of a cross,
its lacework
a system of streams
wound into stone—

grapes and pomegranates
pomegranates and grapes
pulpy in my hands.

Palmettos sawed my palms.
A rising moon in the moss-grown
stone mirrored the light

where winged griffins,
those talismans of blood
flew into the arms of Christ.

Down a gully,
like a volute,

I found a way
to the dry clay

of the border,
where a scimitar
cut the horizon.

Pegasus flew
out of the tufa walls
into the white shroud of Ararat

and the ringing bells
slid into the scree.

Down there I felt my name
disappear.

Lowlands

"North Sea's just over there,"
the Flemish waitress said. You can see
everywhere but you can't see anything,

then the headlights make the fog a little gold
the way the maples turn in my yard
back in the upstate valley

where my son dives in a leaf pile
on his way to school with his friends,
and I keep turning his ritual over in my mind:

two pills of chemo at night,
6 MP it's called, so familiar now like a ham and cheese sandwich.
Tomorrow when I drive north to Bruges, he'll get his shot

of methotrexate—nutriphils, platelets, the invisible
hooks between cells. On my book tour in Amsterdam
an Indonesian journalist asked me how

genital contact could bring a President down.
Histerica Passio dragged our quarry down.
"Isn't that Yeats?" she asked. We giggled but just kept

the tape going. Through the window the canals shined
like they were varnished,
and I could see the lines beginning to form in front

of the Anne Frank House already at 8:30.
The charm of the brown brick
like something out of Vermeer—an absurdity,

as if it were a gloss
on the idea of Jews hiding out in the suffocating dark.
A girl your daughter's age menstruating there.

It comes back to me now the first time I heard that word
at 10, when my mother explained it to me.
Menses. Why girls bleed at 13.

I was startled but gratified by her honesty,
for bringing me one step closer to life.
To the body and its order.

And for whatever reason
no one can tell me why the shut-off
switch of the white cells breaks down.

The cool opaque light of Vermeer falls on the brick.
A little piece of blue heaven, Anne Frank
called her secret annex.

Cool daylight on Herengracht.
When the window opens
there's a gilded coat of arms,

some chinoiserie, brass studs in a Spanish chair.
In the midst of the carnage
of the Dutch war for independence

the painters of the lowlands
reduced the world to the folds in a woman's skirt,
a wineglass of seduction, the rhyming shapes of trees,

cloth & bread & wicker;
a room could be a camera obscura.
To be able to move freely, to have some help

with my work again at last, Anne wrote, *in other words, school.*
I carry the image around: my son
diving on a pile of leaves in the maple light—

Sleeping waters and calm streams
consume the borders, goes the Armenian proverb.
I had no answer for the Indonesian journalist.

I couldn't explain the history of impeachment
or Monica Lewinsky. Was it too easy to focus on the
way light hardens around a pear in a bowl,

or spreads from a knife
on the edge of a table
before it returns to a vanishing point?

In the backyard the light settles on
piles of gold leaves, my son and his friend Max
chuck a rake into a blue spruce

laughing at the fish-shape dangling
from the bough. The poplars rise into the Flemish blue
and the sea's more than a sound in the mind.

Night Patio

1

Because I took the oath
of Styx in the baby-boom stream

and went to Mount Rushmore, where I looked
at the faces and didn't turn to stone,

I walk in the red glow of a TV tower

under the shadow of a Coke bottle.

2

If May is gone with its flaming
tulips,

June turns the night sky-blue,

and a tree opens and the bees spill from its side.

3

While the videos
send their gray-blue light into the night

I dream back to the silver egg
glowing in my parents' yard in Teaneck, New Jersey, 1951,
as the 2×4s of the split-levels settle,

and the DNA twists like a rope ladder
around a tree—

the air's a breeze—
and Peggy Lee's "Fever"
is radioactive on the Dial-Beam.

4

In the third ward of Englewood Hospital
where my father attended

the kids of Bergen County
and the old Armenian women
who lived on yams and wine

because the Turks had turned
their boys to dust,

the shadow met me too.

5

So on my patio at the century's end

a cloud of blue light,
like the glow
of a Power Mac screen

came lower than the cornice
of my house—a click of the mouse—
and a flat midwest voice came through the bleeping:

"Secrecy is a decision, I'm a Baptist anyway.

We were wrapped in Cut-Rite, right into the Trinity

over Alamogordo
mountains flared like aluminum foil

Stimson, Glover, Byrnes

(Oppenheimer was a coward.)

I kept hearing in my head
Vive le President Wilson, vive le capitaine d'artillerie américain

"saw the heavens fill with commerce,
argosies of magic sails."

Little Boy. It's good to be a kid, drink Cherry Coke
and watch the cottonwood pods blow apart
as the train flies past Independence.

You do it. You do it. You do it.

The Jap War's over. You're free."

6

As the matrix dots dissolved
and the gutter swilled with breeze,
the sight of a bird

whose head was bright as Venus
appeared on the cedar shingles.

"August 6. A saké bottle was clear air.
My desk opened into eyes that run down a face.

At night the beautiful cirrus limbs
floated like a helix past—

We're the streaks of the ICBMs
as they tethered
over Iowa,

where a box top of Cheerios
gets you a plastic A-bomb ring.

I want to tell you how a morning spelling lesson
is."

7

A cloud of fireflies
like patio orange dripped

into the black. I dropped my
bag of Doritos and my diet Sprite
and this brassy voice poured out—

"The sound bites of the plastic wheel,
that's how we loved you and you loved me and Desi,
even more than Ike and Mamie.

You'll know too, the way an elbow pops from a socket, you'll
know—

I wasn't Red as McCarthy claimed.
You'll know when your sponsors are off the air.

Norman Vincent Peale, J. Edgar Hoover and *TV Guide*.

You'll know the self-
reflexive heart of Desilu,
hung like a charm

from the neck of America,
where no one returns without a pistol
cigarette-lighter and their children burned."

for Robert Jay Lifton

Ellis Island

The tide's a Bach cantata.
The beach is the swollen neck of Isaac.

The tide's a lamentation of white opals.
The beach is free. The Coke machine rusted out.

Here is everything you'll never need:

hemp-cords, curry-combs, jade and musk,
a porcelain cup blown into the desert—

stockings that walked to Syria in 1915.

On the rocks some ewes and rams
graze in the outer dark.

The manes of the shoreline undo your hair.
A sapphire ring is fingerless.

The weed and algae are floating like a bed,
and the bloodless gulls—

whose breaths would stink of all of us
if we could kiss them on the beaks—

are gnawing on the dead.

Train to Utica

And then the Hudson
overcame the wheels of the train
and when the lights went out

the cell phones began bleeping—
laser green like fireflies
in the hands of passengers.

"We just gonna stay here a while till
Motha Naycha run her cawse,"
the conductor's voice soft.

The black woman next to me
turned up her boom box

and the Supremes were smooth
like *Baby love, baby love.*

And then as if out of the holes
in the after-glare of the ceiling light
Le Huyen's voice floated into the car

that's just capitalist music—love and privacy, ya know.

★

At dawn I left the refugee center in Utica.
Drove through arson-gutted neighborhoods
as the parolees were milling around in the sifted blue-gray light.

Ya know what it means to be con lai?

Donna and Beulah were the big ones I remembered.
They blew billboards down on Route 4,
ripped the scoreboard from the high school field.

This one Floyd—male and furious—from
some tropical depression beyond a wall of clouds;
mid-September, northeast America.

*Diana Ross was the banned voice of the colonial oppressor,
I sneaked her in on my Walkman while I was selling every-
thing from Honda generators to sugar cane juice to push brooms.*

Operation Babylift it was called.
A mother in Saigon; a father from Ohio
5/4 Artillery, 5th Division

*I didn't have a coat in the monsoon rains,
just a Coca-Cola T-shirt. High Pumas and blue jeans.*

When the trees fell on the tracks
the woman behind me began to cry,
and only the sound of the buzz saws

of the Coast Guard crew calmed her.
"Soon we'll be free," she whimpered.

★

In the glare of cell-phone light on the window,
I saw hummingbirds in the mango blossoms,
a Buddhist temple in a cashew grove

the voice of a metal drum drifted out—
over the tamarinds and plantains
down to the Mekong River

where the sampans were loaded with
rice and corpses and green lotus shoots

the hummingbirds blurred
in the yellow flowers of Tet.

English sounded like barking dogs,
I learned it from Lucille Ball and Fonzie

*

We backed down the river after midnight
snaking through Yonkers and Riverdale
along the West Side Highway

until we disappeared underground
where the sewage pipes angled
and emptied into the groaning generators

T-shirts were stacked on the dock
in bright sun, Ronald Wilson Reagan
Insane Anglo Warlord *on the back.*

It was important for con lai to wear them.
I wore mine every day. But still it was
like Marguerite Duras' L'Amant.

I lived on swamp grass and fish bones.
I was wrapped in the saffron robe of a Buddhist nun,
my mind cut in half by the rolling wheel.

Outside Penn Station,
the asphalt was like a soft, wet field
as I walked toward a cab.

In the street-light glare
of a Korean grocery
some yellow flowers shined

a sheet blew off a man sleeping
on the curb and flailed
down the vault of 34th Street.

for Jane and Hugh Pinchin

The Children's Museum at Yad Vashem

I walk across some stones.
The day is blue-tiled light.
The sun is sealed across.

My mother leads me by the hand
into the den of names.
I walk across some stones.

The mirror is black.
The candles have laughing faces.
The sun is sealed across.

My mother turns into dust.
My hand disappears.
I walk across some stones.

A scroll of a viola is a Nazi cross;
the sky is a cave of faces
that fly into the sun sealed across.

I follow my mother into the mirror.
The sun erupts on one candle.
I walk across some stones,
and the sun is sealed across.

Harpert, Revisited

Russian thistle, glasswort, sarsazan;
the air in late September cooling,
dew burning off the fescue by eight.

In the absence hovering over
the earth-graves, over the calcium
that won't dissolve, you were honeysuckle,

and cotoneaster growing
over some vaguely recognizable
khatchgar in a field where the goats graze.

Out on the steppe, where I first found you,
the thyme and lavender
were drying faintly scented.

Your father slipped through
just north of Harpert on Lake Goljuk
on his way to the Dersim.

Hackberry, hawthorn, terebinth.
When I say each name, each sound
goes nowhere into the dead Turkish air.

The American consul, Davis, wrote,
At least 10,000 on the lake shore; covered with a few
shovelfuls of dirt, the gendarmes found it easier to do this

than to dig holes. One could see the arms or legs
or even the heads sticking out of the ground.
A few hungry-looking cats were prowling around.

The Five Satins were doo-wopping on
CD, and the figs and the champagne
were just right.

The water was Adirondack clear,
and nothing but a crane disappeared in the cliff.
Our mouths and teeth on each other.

Most of them had been partially eaten by dogs.
Fragments of bones and clothing . . .
Unburned. One red fez was conspicuous.

Outside the stone fortress, the rooks
and hawks swooping down. Your head
appearing, disappearing in the light.

Tracer in the tree ring, isotopic, half-life—
stay here with me in the evening light.

Parable for Vanished Countries

The mountain was close.
Far. Then closer.
Rivulets of light ran across it.

Lakes were white circles,
then canyons,
then empty eyes.

The sky was a field of burning stones.
It was neither day nor night.
It was jasmine, and fires went out

over my head. The closer I got,
the farther it was.
Rivers pooled like green wax,

and the orchards and vineyards
on its flanks flared
like the wings of a scarlet tanager.

The trees glared like shepherds' crooks
in the brass light; crows roosted on them,
and the mountain rose into the sky,

until it was a cloud
shimmering in black air.

Jade Boat

The Esso signs were spliced by gulls and creosote.
Newark was a track of hypodermic glass,
Bayonne floated by on a misconnection.

A good fastball high inside can deck a man.
And then some bungalows rose from the cattails
and Perth Amboy was the past.

When the sand was visible
and the birds rose out of the beery foam,
we sprayed the dashboard with some cans of Schlitz.

Oh Maybelline, why can't you be true . . .
Oh Maybelline—like a warped wind off Kalaloch

where the tide undresses starfish
bleeding and magenta on the rocks, and the urchins
spread their green hairs to lip the air.

The soul's a wicked slider
breaking the way the road did into bushed-out dunes
south of Barnegat Light,

where my dashboard glistened with dry foam
and the fog began to set,
and the lighthouse was a jade boat

where birds circled—desperate, squawking
as if the fish should jump
into their prayer.

for Richard Hugo

FROM *DYER'S THISTLE*
(1996)

August Diary

8/1

From here groomed fields and clumps of trees,
a silo of corrugated tin and a white barn blur.

Unseasonable cool days,
high, blue, a few clouds like ripped pillows
as if this were a lip of the North Sea

and I could look out and imagine Denmark.
But I'm in my office three floors up.

8/3

In Armenian there's a word—*garod*—rhymes with "maud."

The beautiful ones are not faithful
and the faithful ones are not beautiful—

a student said that about some Pavese translations,
here in my office.

Should I tell you what *garod* means?

8/5

What's happening in Spitak and Sarajevo and the West Bank
is splayed like the cortex of a silicon chip in the fuzzy air.

Maria, the physician from Armenia, was 25 & had one plastic arm
and one real arm. I met her in East Hampton on the deck of a house
      on the dunes.
After the earthquake she had no husband,
no parents, and only one child.

"I'm in a good mood today," she said, "let's talk about
something else." I poured her an Amstel Light.

8/10

The coolness intrudes—
month of wind-sprints and retching for the coach.
It comes back like nerve ends after surgery.

Along a country road cicadas rattling.
Chicory and sweet pea intruding on the ripe barley.

I picked up some seed packs from a junk shop on Rt. 20,
a tomato blazed in red ink/ 1926, Fredonia, N.Y.

8/11

What's between us? The red ink of the tomato?

How does an image stay? Or is it always aftermath?
The way deep black reflected the most light in Talbot's first calotypes.

But *garod:* tongue of a snake,
meaning exile, longing for home.

Thomas Wedgwood got images by getting sunlight
to pass through things onto paper brushed with silver nitrate:

wings of a dragonfly, the spine of an oak leaf—
fugitive photograms. But he couldn't stop the sun
until it turned the paper black.

Stop the light before it goes too far?

Or is desire what *garod* means?
Longing for a native place.

8/17

Maria said she was learning how to connect nerve endings
in the hand so hands and arms would work again.
There were so many in Armenia without working hands and arms.

At the end of each dendrite is a blurred line
like the horizon I'm squinting.

Image of the other:
light-arrested; not the image of ourselves.

8/21

After digging scallions one day Dickinson defined freedom:
Captivity's consciousness, so's liberty.

Maybe *garod* is about the longing for the native place
between two selves.

8/22

I love the brute force of silence in Roger Fenton's
Sebastopol from Cathcart's Hill, 1855. The Crimean inner war.

The artlessness of silver is like my tongue in your wet space,
or like the news photos that bring us the pressure of disaster.

Beloved topography,
garod then must mean yearning.

Is that how we loved under the rattling Nippon porcelain,
in the light calotyped by the fire escape?

8/25

garod: the grain chute that spills
into a dark barn which is endless,

like the self when it's out of reach.

Are we so lonely that a constellation
could blacken and fill up that same barn,

and that be me or you?

But still we're piss and oats and stock in there.
We're like civet, who wouldn't love it.

8/31

the new glass-plate pictures:
transparent as air, Szarkowski wrote

like windows

the fragmentary, scruffy, particularity
of real living behind them—

Physicians

1

Above school kids in Episcopal
jackets cherubs are singing
to the beautiful fake lapis
of St. John the Divine

and from this side chapel
I see through the blue
to the 6th floor of St. Luke's
where my father's heart caved in.

In the thirties my grandfather
made his rounds three floors down.
In the weak sun the black rocks
by a shepherd's robe seem piled

like fat medical texts
or small suitcases full of Dickens
in German my grandfather translated
to learn English so he could pass

his exam in the Empire State,
to use his silver instruments
on the eyes ears nose and throat.

In a snapshot he's large-eyed, glazed,
as if he should've followed
his cousin, the Bishop, to a cave.

Instead he climbed down
the catastrophes of New World
faces, the warped shapes
that flare up the senses.

Tubes lit in the throat.
The auscultated fog
of the ear tuned
to pass the pitches

of the world. I think of him
scoping the cochlea,
that purgatory
where the screech

of a yellow Checker
and the mute twittering
of Satchmo's horn
were white light.

Down the ducts of joy and pain
my grandfather called tears
(not *lachrymae Christi*),
but the fissure between two continents

that sent him with Armenia's
refugees along the junked canals,
the Dardanelles, the Atlantic.

Eye to eye with a lens,
he could see the retina's
orange spot,
and it was a floating nation.

On a clean metal table
the empty whites stared back,
like marbles flickering

in Turkish moonlight.
The piles of Armenian corpses
he tended in Adana he carried
in the tremor of his hand.

2

A dark plane slicing Zurbarán's pears.
The ripe light in the bell-end
of Cézanne's pear strokes,

the honey-colored viols
weighing down a tree of life.
My father pointed these out in museums.

But in that pear-shaped organ
from which the raucous parrots flew,
in that fruit of blood

soaking in the vaults of the chest,
my father worked.

If you could loose your love to flow
down there in the eddies that swell and shrink

against the barnacled and moss-spun bulkheads
you would see the contradictions
in the oscillations of the unstillable red sea.

Amidst envelopes of membranes
venous trunks and a splay
of filaments which wire a pump to the head

my father could be a man of adamant
tying his terror in a Windsor knot,
pressing it to the icy starch of his shirt.

I could tell on certain days he'd felt
the inward suck,
the vortex where men and women disappear.

In the final seconds, he'd say,
"the heart's a bag of worms,
then it's all calm,"

and slip into his formal chair
distant as blue light;
ask for salt and bread
and water without ice.

My Father on the Berengaria, 1926

The sky like the red silk of the fortune-teller
in Bucharest. Diesel fuel.
Things rise here.

The letters flying like swans on the passport,
République d'Arménie. I've never been there,
is it a country?

Gulls squawk into the dirty sun.
A refugee is a free person.
Mother said "yes, yes."

She said "when the lights go out,
don't be afraid, we're here."
And the train rocked like the wind had arms,

over the trellised rumbles,
over the olive grove and the wool and garlic.

Constantinople floated away like the sun
on cups of waves the color of pee.

In the shade of the Arc de Triomphe
we had cones of lemon ice.
"There's more of that in New York."

When I crawl through the wet cotton
and the hemp and leather of the hull,
I smell Lucia's hair in my room.

Dark air is the inside of a brass urn.
I have the neck of a swan in my hand.
I'm twine. I'm breathing.

World War II

My mother worked
for Irvington Varnish
south of Newark where
her sister lived

in a room writing
like Katherine Anne Porter.
My mother wore goggles
and a white coat

to earn college tuition.
In Budapest Eichmann mulled
over 200 tons of tea,
2,000 cases of soap;

Jews for supplies.
My mother was gloved past
her wrists rigging
polyester for parachutes.

The shadow of a poplar
on the wall was the hand
of the Turkish wind.
My grandmother feared

my mother would disappear
into the brick buildings
of the college catalog.
Topf & Sons made vans

in '43, and the waste
was slight as it slid

into the Bug River.
Bucknell University

was a dark copse
past the Delaware Water Gap
where Turkish gendarmes
emerged in the daylight.

My mother boxed khaki
and flint; a hand
placed electrodes on
my grandmother's head,

and the grackles
in Upper Silesia ate
powdery ash on the oaks.

Ions: a convulsive seizure,
ECT they called it,
and my aunt slept on
A Ship of Fools in a run-

down room in Belmar.
On cool sheets in the evening
when the poplar shadow
disappeared, my grandmother rested

and my mother returned
from work, when the sun
on the oil drums of the Pike
was pure acetylene

like a road out of Armenia,
out of Turkey, out of Treblinka
out of New Jersey.

The Oriental Rug

I

I napped in the pile
in the brushed and bruised
Kashan on our living room floor
an eight-year-old sleeping

in vegetable dyes—
roots and berries,
tubers, shafts, dry leaves

the prongy soil
of my grandparents' world:
eastern Turkey, once Armenia.

The wine-red palmettes
puckered with apricot buds
and fine threads of green
curling stem-like over my cheek

leaving a shadow like filigree
on my eye as I closed it.

The splintering green wool
bled from juniper berries
seemed to seep, even then,

into the wasp-nest cells
breathing in their tubular ways
inside my ear and further back.

*

On certain nights
when the rain thrummed
against the clapboard

and my father's snoring issued
down the hall, I slept on the rug
curled and uncovered
and the sea of ivory

between the flowers
undulated as if the backs
of heavy sheep were breathing
in my mouth.

The prickly cypress
down by the friezed border
spiraled in my night gazing.
Armenian green:

dwarf cabbage, shaded cedar,
poppy stem, the mossy pillow
where my grandfather
sat in the morning dark

staring at the few goats
that walked around the carnage.
Outside my house the grass
never had such color.

II

Now I undo the loops
of yarn I rested my head on.
Under each flower
a tufted pile loosens.

I feel the wool give way
as if six centuries of feet
had worn it back to the hard
earth floor it was made to cover.

Six centuries of Turkish heels
on my spine-dyed back:
madder, genista, sumac—
one skin color in the soil.

I lose myself
in a flawed henna plant
jutting toward the scroll.
Its rose-pink eyes burst

off the stems.
The auburn dust
which reddens the women
returns with a sharp wind.

The vine of lily-blossoms winding
by the fringe once shined
like fur when a spray of sun
flushed through a curtain—

that gracious shape hardens now
like a waxy twig at summer's end.

I hear wind running
through heart-strings.

I hear an untuned zither
plucked by a peacock's accidental strut.

Warp and weft come undone;
sludge spills back to the earth

(my liver's bitter
as the pomegranate's acid seed).

III

The heavy mallet a Parsee boy
once used to beat the knots
beneath the pile so
the weft would disappear

vibrates in me
as a knelling bell
over the Sea of Marmara
once rang toward the West.

I pitch myself
into the spinning corolla
of an unnamed flower

coral, red, terra-cotta,
get thrown down a lattice of leaves

to the dark balm
of the marshy hillsides

of my faraway land—
the poppied acres
of Adoian's hands.

IV

I pry my way
into a rose—
undoing its blighted cliché.

I strain for the symmetry
of its inflorescence,

slide along the smooth
cup of a petal
till I rush headfirst
down the pistil

feeling the tubey walls
muscle me to the ovary
where a bee was swooning
on some pollen.

Wrapped this tight
I suck my way into the nectaries;
feel a hummingbird's tongue
and the chalky wing of a moth.

That wet, I wash
to the cool leaflets,
rim their toothed edges,
then back-rub

the remains of sepals
which kept the rose alive
in blighted April when Adana
and Van were lopped off the map.

I come apart in the thorn
(the spiky side that kept the jackal out)
and disperse whatever's left
of me to the earth.

V

I walk with a rug on my back.
Become to myself a barren land.
Dust from the knots
fills my arms

and in the peaceful New World sun
becomes fine spume.

A sick herbalist
wandering in a century
mapped by nations wandering.

The dyes come through the wool,
break the grid of threads
holding the shapes to form:

safflower, my Dyer's Thistle,
carry me on your burr
so I may always feel
dry gusts on my neck.

Kermes, dried like a scab,
crush me to your womanly scarlet chest.
I feel your scales
flutter in my eyes.

Madder root—
which makes the red of Karabagh
bleed along one long hallway.

Tyrian purple, from a mollusk shell
lodged in Phoenician sand—
gurgle all your passion in my ear.

for my daughter, Sophia

Duck 'n' Cover, 1953

A shadow of a bough
hangs on the wall like a headless mutt.
Tic-Tac-Toe of the windows,
then maples like gold lamps.

We start with "My country 'tis of thee,"
and end with the Lord our Shepherd.
Out of the light blue
that siren makes us deaf.

Kimchee makes my father sick.

We know what to do.
We don't stumble on a shoe,
or move our pencils from the beveled grooves.

The nap of my crew cut bristles my knees.
I look at shoes and the shadows of leaves.

The light spills like a brook
into the seams of rocks.

Korea's a sky-blue thumb on our map above the sink.
The floorboards shine like honey.

Patent leather. Saddles. Bucks. Buster Browns.
There's a saying that passes among us like water—
put your head between your legs and kiss your ass good-bye.

The Y in my alphabet soup floated toward the Yalu.

Then we sit again on our maple chairs
bright as yellow jackets.

Flat Sky of Summer

In a salt-rutted
scooped-out side of a dune,
I curled around a picture book,
skinny and burnt brown as a beetle.

Staring through the glare
of the midday sun,
hot enough to scatter
my puffy white friends

I thumbed those pages
in the rank wind
like a slow boy
learning to read.

I dropped down
a Minoan bowl;
drew into the gray and red
folds of its coil

rested on the dry
thumb-rubbed bottom
hearing water splash.

In the sandstone of Ur
bits of shell
laid-in purple rock,

or the curly-headed
straight-nosed boy
playing his double flute

to the berry-winged bushes
in the tan silence
of a wall in Tarquinia

chalk and dust
on my tongue.

★

In the chips of gold (more real to me
than the science fiction of Revelation),
in the nimbus over the pear-shaped head
of Christ—a sun within a sun

on the high lunette of Holy Wisdom
beyond the hammers of Iconoclasts,

in the flat gold-leaf sky
of the Armenian past

on vellum the color of sheep's milk

a teal bird—
a red twig in its beak—
flew out at me.

★

The half-globe of a breast
caressed by the shadow of an odalisque.
Almond dust on Sephardic eyes,

a thigh of broken light
scattering Modigliani's head,

Vincent's tongue
drying in the windless heat of Aix,

the sun needling the poplars,
Uccello's lancers soaring
in the quills of hawks and eagles
above the pressure of the wind;

off diaphanous plumes of white
a breeze of turpentine
apricots and cherries bleeding
on the Gorky-green world,

a magenta iris blooming in the stomach,
snails and worms crawling
in the blood's sugary sediment;

out of the sand-brown ground on my hands
a butter churn, a clay baking tub,
the Kazak's sun-cured scarlet,

and where the lavender trees grew out
of the lake's white salt
I saw the heraldic branches in the yellow light
of Toros Roslin's mind—

I felt a twitter in the visible world.

Rock 'n' Roll

The groove in black vinyl got deeper

What was that light?

A migrant
I slid into a scat,

and in the purple silk
and the Canoe

there was sleekness and a rearview mirror.

And the Angels flew out of the cloisonné vase.
They were the rachitic forks hanging in the midnight kitchen.
And so I called you after the house was still.
My turquoise Zenith melting

And you asked: What was that light?

I was spinning. I was the trees shivering,
and the snake of coiled light on the ceiling
was moonglow.

I wasn't a fool in a satin tux.
I was Persian gold and blue chenille
I was the son of the Black Dog of Fate.

I said: I saw a rainbow of glass
above the Oritani Theater.

Lord, lead me from Hackensack, New Jersey
into the white streak of exhaust.

Saigon / New Jersey

It was russet light, Orchard Lane,
white-shingle colonials

and the *ch ch* of the sprinklers,
small rainbows in twilight,

the fabric smell
of funeral parlor on us

From a fence we fell
to the fairway on all fours,

a sky of purple berries,
my hand swollen from a doubleheader,

Ho Chi Minh, a tin sound in the air.

A brash oak casket
was less than the absence

of your brother's arm still clear
as the ghostly rubber of the mound.

Your Heaven Scent heavy
as we slid into the trap,

and the white number of the flag
grew incandescent. You who loved

the classics said Orion's eyes
were wild birds against pure black,

then our tongues failed
and we burned into each other.

Out of School

When the cheerleaders faded
and the oaks were stripped

Sunday was a worn sky
in which a ball was blunt

as a faded moon, austere like
going steady. A text unglued

and names and dates crammed
in drudgery fell out. Carthage

was desolate, and Caesar humped
his polished legions past the Rhone.

On the winding bands of Trajan's
Column the Parthians were screwed

to the foul mouth of posterity,
felicitas saeculi—

bits of color flickered
on the ceiling of my room,

and Dylan's a cappella rose
through curlicues of smoke

over the college flags
of *veritas* on the wall.

I listened till my ear was numb
and the face of Hattie Carol

was black wax like those horses
turning into history.

First Communion

Mother of God. The wine lusted
on my lips. Weeks and weeks
in the world.

It was a rainy morning in May.
The forget-me-nots still powder blue,
odorless, clean with yellow eyes.

I stood outside the closed curtain.
The ceiling hung like a chalice
of air.

I knelt in wet clothes
and a cloud rose over me.
Ashes. Myrrh. The oblations.

Without deceit or wiles the rain
came in sheets, blurring the windows.
A place without doors.

Woodstock

In the mud of a tire rut,
    we were the filaments.

We said if Mrs. Agnew could make music
    on Spiro's flute

we said the clubs in the hands of the Chicago cops
    would liquefy.

The trees shook with the throb of steel.

What did we do to be so red, white, and blue?

We were inexorable
    like the dialectic unraveling from Hanoi
        to the Jacksonian grass.

We were the inebriates of vitamin C and cocaine,
the daughters of the gray flannel suit.

And when the shaman spread his yellow robe like the sun
he was all teeth and amp

and what were we?

Last Days Painting (August 1973)

The plain air above the Palisades,
the blue anonymous egg,

can you make chromos by electric light?

I couldn't tell sun from stone,
Tenafly's varnished light
from the rambles around Hoboken—

for instance Lancon, Lemud, Daumier, Gavarni
and Bodmer remind one more of piano playing.
Millet is perhaps a solemn organ.

Against the static clouds,
a gull in the bourbon light

a nude descending
the sky comes to its knees on the rocks,
and if the things that emerge

are black and gray
and if the unpretentious gulls fly into them
I could be chalk.

Descending: surveillance of the visible
like Nixon, and the face caught on
the horizontal band of the old Magnavox.

You could say that somewhere between
Masaccio and Alexander Portnoy is the truth.
I lost my head up there

in a satiny roundel, like the sun's pucker.
I wanted to make the crêpe de chine
of her slip into a cloud

unraveling in summer rain
so she could really fly.
Descending: Watergate, denouement, worm's eye.

I envy the Japanese the extreme clearness
which everything has in their work, simple as breathing.

★

Can't trust what's in a tube.
Take gum resin from a plum tree.
Cut it up, put it in an earthenware pot,

add water and put in the sun.
Stir carefully, strain through a cloth and grind
all pigments with it. Saffron: from the dried stigma

of a crocus. Theophilus used the pigment for making tin look
like gold, but clear yellow glass too.
That's what I wanted. Clear yellow glass,

so that things could be seen like the steel
of a Chevy in the cement and iron of the
collapsed West Side Highway

or the rusty light gleaming
from the sterns of the Cunard liners
in the filthy harbor;

it's why I believed in Heade;
his canvas as if the world were a glass
dish, silvered by an amalgam

let down into the well until it grazed
the surface of something
and everything came back like a raised ornament:

trees, rocks, a boy, a canoe, a straw hat.
Heade's America: Vietnam reversed.
Fifty years hence nobody will wish to go back

to this period, or if there follows a time
of antiquated decay or so-called
time of perukes and crinolines,

people will be too dull to think about
it at all; if there comes a change for the better, tant mieux.

*

If you look at van der Weyden's sky
behind the cross, it's a void—
a place of the Buddha, as if our inspiration

reflex were reversed and the self
imploding with nothingness could see.

Today I'm a bright casualty
on the verge of something new
as when desire marries the skyline,

clean, and unaugmented, like the hem
of God's robe—where the world
is no longer the tooth of a gargoyle.

Go there.

Post Vietnam

Hecuba

Did I nurse for nothing?
Were my women too wild
when they combed their bracelets
on Polymestor's face?

I stalked MacArthur till
his slate face sank in the Yalu.
Saw Westmoreland lose an eye at Da Nang.

From my burnt-out sockets
l see Botha's car
crystal clear as a Caddy.

Andromache

I used to watch the crows,
like dads and lads in the trees
of their countries.

I used to genuflect,
now I'm custard.

The iron wheel's Hector's head.

I've split for a place
north of Tonkin,

my breasts
are Venetian glass.

American Dreaming

1

I rowed through rushes.
Root-knees and loops
barely breathing,

maggots lisping,
bubbles breaking.

Spikes and bristles brushed
my arms,
and the reeds' pith split,

and spindles of air rose.

2

Heard a foot in sludge—

a sound like an Armenian word.

3

At Sandy Hook,
the lighthouse spoked the air,
as if wicks still burned
in spermaceti.

In the wave-washed paths
of lobsterbacks,
in the reservoir of blood-money

Hessian smoke
kept blowing into the junk-

stone towers
in the British sediment.

Fog wrapped my head.
The light was straight
as a gull's wing cutting the air

and water slid like a black eel
through weirs and hooks of grass,

and the sounds of familiar names

Hackensack, Ho-Ho-Kus, Fort Lee
Passaic, Engle wood, Ten a fly

lodged in a channeled whelk.

A thud of European muskets
in the air,

and memory's a sieve for Delaware skulls
to pour like powder.

As the flint-heads
were swallowed by the waves,

I saw the white
scarless, fog-wrapped beach

and the shreds of breechcloth
unstitched from Pontiac's flag

beneath the plastic cups
from the luncheonettes and beach vendors.

4

In the stench of chub heads
and the trailing skirts of air,
my gaze

gave way to Armenian silt—
the cradle in the crook'd
neck of the Tigris

where a crone rowed
out of a corset
into the pleated reeds:

the linen stiff with sun
on the sandstone like parchment
in a silent place.

In the rice's chiming pale
a black partridge ruffled water.

Lost tea and filaments of silk
settled in my throat.

Shrunken beds,
once Armenian trade routes,
were fissures in the palm.

Corpses floated
like bloated goat skin.

Apricots dried to ears.
Almonds blanched
to eyes.

5

As the moonlight parted fog,
the way the sun shifts

steam in a Turkish bath,
that scouring light glittered
on black water,

and the air
was a broadsword.

I watched the light rinse the surface
and diminish like the white string of a kite,
and rowed back to the bulrushes

imagining their slick piths
holding my two waters together.

Mandelstam in Armenia, 1930

Between arid houses and crooked streets
a shadow could be your wife or a corpse
and a mule's hooves sounded like Stalin's
fat fingers drumming a table.

In the Caucasus eagles and hawks
hung in the blue's basilica.
A swallow flew off a socle
into the wing of an echo—

history's caw and chirp and bird shit
on the tombs in the high grass.
On hairy serrated stems
poppies flagged like tongues.

Petals of flat paper
lined your thumbed-out pockets.
Anther seeds burned your pen.

From a cloud of broom a red bee stumbled
to your fish-globe brain.
A casket of light kissed the eyebrows of a tree.

Lake Sevan's rippling blue skirt
lapped you. Slime tongues got your eyes.
A half-dead perch slithered your ear.

When the evening air settled
on the creatures of the mountain
the sun was the Virgin's head.

Here, where the bush grew with fresh blood
and ancient thorns, you picked the rose
without scissors. Became an omen.

Geese Flying Over Hamilton, New York

That's how I woke
to a window of chalk sky

like indifference, like the sheet wrapped
around two people,

and the radio sounded like fuzz
on a boom mike,

the rhetoric needling in about the dead in Croatia

then the light came and the branch
of a sycamore on the wall
    was the menorah
on the Arch of Titus

I was thinking like

the cows by the paddock in a peel of sun

when they cut a wide arrow—
their feathers oily with tundra,
the gabbling like field-holler.

I looked out to the Fisher-Price toys
blue and yellow in fog,

silver light, gauche on the spruces,

and the words Pol Pot
the geese chromatic, then gone.

Phnom Penh static like snow the day may bring,
like a monsoon sweeping over a menorah

like the falling barn seeming to rise in white air.

When the spruces lose their shape
later in the purple air

my daughter will flick a switch,
and a stuffed chair will be a place for light to coalesce.

After dinner and a bottle of good Bordeaux
the sky floats like a numb pillow of radar.

Down here the dark is warm
like ordinary death.

The Backyard

Out of blueness,
the hummingbird in the privet.
Then silence shafts the sky:
and you can hear

a cat yawning,
missiles moving to Griffiss,
a scarf of chartreuse
drying like a caterpillar.

The seeds in the heart
are like plovers lost inland.
Don't try flying with them.
Just feel the lift,

and the horizon
is raspberries
fermenting in the shed.

But then the hummingbird's gone
and the air is a flask
for the henna-tulips . . .

coils of amber
go up in powder

and neither a twig
nor the obelisk of a birch
can measure a distance.

A Toast

A branch smooth as the rubbed foot of Saint Peter,
puce, porous, rinsed by wind.
Clean spear of a skeleton.
Bridge of a Roman nose.
Cask of air.

When I walk into that croft,
the trees at my back like a reredos
carved by rain,

then the day could pour like ouzo
into my crystal thimble—
a shot of air for friendship,
a bar of bleached light

for the necklace of stones
strung on the chalky ridges—
a blackbird smearing the trees
for our daughters in the alizarin of day.

Then, a swallow could hook
its neck on a rafter,
a hawk mistake a lure
for God and Country,

I wouldn't know—
my shot glass
a splintered flock of feathers
in the wind.

for Bruce Smith

My Son Stares into a Tulip

*Language is the replacement for
the separation from the mother.*
                —after Lacan

He was nuzzling
in the grass I had just cut.
Crushed bluebells on his palms.

He nudged a few inches
like a caterpillar or something amphibious
and then caught by accident

his hand on the ha-ha,
and so braced his pale, slightly bowed legs,
to bring himself upright

for the first time, I think,
in his life,

and found himself face to face
with a tulip, which was falling

apart from a week of sun
and a recent harsh shower,

and so its black stain
was like sticky dye.

I watched him stare into it.

In the house his mother's
breasts—the crab apples of September
drying up.

If words could fill the
gap in his life
each petal would become a tongue,

each black anther
a stalk of light.

I hope his upright grasp
of the green stem holds him
when he's fallen back to ground.

I hope a breeze descends
on him out of the blue.

Morning News

Through a glass door
    a pheasant grousing the snow,
through the maples

a Baptist spire
    in the blue Adirondack sun.
Purring from the Krups.

On my wall a small map of the flat earth
    Hic Dragones; an open mouth
of cobalt like terra incognita.

I think of Elizabeth Bishop's map:
    raspberry, shadowed green
exotic peasants like *the moony Eskimo*

and the conceit of countries
    Norway's hare
spills into the furrows of laid paper.

My son who is 1
    waddles in like a drunk
in his blue corduroys

presses a button:
chrominance, luminance, synchronization:

a shadow mask. Phosphors:
    yellow   red   blue

the Berlin Wall
    a dam of people—
windows of a split-level

in east Belfast blown out,
     a woman, a teenager
really, slips into jeans

tight as silk on her ass;
     then a bottle of beer
frothing over the shaft.

A man in a suit
     goes on reading a cue
about bottles crushed/

the throats of farmers . . .
     my son
tripping pulls the plug

and my daughter flings open
     the sliding glass door—
a little meadow of snow

glistens then melts
     into her hair,
the color of Smyrna figs,

she runs to the TV
     puts the plug in—
a new station comes up.

The End of the Reagan Era

Endless horizons of wheat and corn
out of Willa Cather's reach,
and Ross Perot moving through it all.

I clicked a lever for my candidate,
the curtains opened like at Oz,
and my vote blew out the doors of the Jehovah's Witness hall.

I walked back through the saffrony maple leaves
just wet enough to stick to my basement trapdoor,
and sat outside and read some student papers on the Gulf War.

I thought of the states floating in their electoral colors
on the screen the way the Scuds and Patriots
flickered in their matrix dots before and after

the Giants played the Bills on Channel 4.
In another century Galileo said, "but still, it moves,"
under his breath, and today the Vatican agrees.

Since legends keep us sane, I think today
of Cianfa, one of the five thieves of Florence,
who was clasped by a six-foot lizard

who ate his nuts and went right up his torso
until the two of them were two-in-one.

I love the clemency of roads this time of year
the way they tail off to the beautiful barns.

In Church

1

In the rheumatic heat of July,
when Public Enemy blared
on the blasters

in a time when arbitrage
and foreign policy
were bureaus of each other,

I made a wrong turn off Broadway
and wound up at St. John the Divine

where I sat in the hot dark
until the traffic died.

★

And a voice comes over
some columns to the breeze of the Golden Horn
over the cypress groves

and flowing bougainvillea
where the bright blue weather and the old
seawalls come together,

where crates of cardamom
and musk are piled and
the cattle hang in blood

above the brass,
where the grain boats
stink and red pleasure

barges drift where Jason
sailed for his fleece—
a voice comes out of the dead water.

In great Sophia
light pours in rosy bars
on the porphyry and the green marble

till the air blooms,
and a chrysalis of lit crosses
makes circles in the air.

Light falls through the lunettes
like arrows of gold that could've
sneaked up the Virgin's dress.

Had the Holy Ghost flitted in
it would've been lost in the glare

and the kiss of peace
Justinian blew from the ambo.

*

Incantations flutter and rhyme
in the apse like wings
in a cloud of incense

thinning on the gold-leafed
vaults where the tongue's vibration
lingers in the upper air,

and rises and rises as if the dome could open
to a half-hemisphere of heaven
where in the translucent glitter of the Kingdom

the Saints are poised in gracious robes
with their thousand-year-frozen faces—
the one truth glued on the grout of their lips.

2

I sit with the incense of memory,
and a bath of dark pours
from the vaults above the pew

Outside, boutiques of money collide
with the street fires in Harlem, whole
skyscrapers are levitated by arbitrage,

and the only inside takeover I can negotiate
is myself in this pew with my herringbone jacket
which I should chuck in the Salvation Army bin

down the block, so I could join the line of choir-
boys in their last innocent ritual
as they stand before the mounted sermon sign

"he shall bring forth judgment unto truth"
(Isaiah 42:3). The Puritans because
they believed God's altar needs not their polish

lifted the boulder of truth higher than the glittering
face of the Nazarene once leaded in glass.

For the spirit they swallowed stones
and shattered all the panes. But beneath the lavender
arch of a Canon Table in an old Gospel

I once tasted the consubstantial dewdrop
in the faded color of a peacock's wing.

So while a stone sinks to the bottom of my
river, a peacock's wing floats by the shore.

Who tells it like it is: Isaiah or Procopius?

3

I started walking backward
down the aisle

when I heard and thought I
saw in the strange fenestration
of that light—

a voice,
first incoherent, and then sharp
as if it were in my ear

There is no reign that executes
justice and judgment;
is that why you whine?

"But Primo Levi's image of a man—
a face that haunts every nation
on the earth—

this, this!"

Don't soak lentils in your mouth.

"Be serious; what's left to praise?"

The fig tree drops rocks
in the morning and the fig
tree drops figs in the morning.

It's your new yard, am I right?
New house, 2 kids, and all that.

"Yup."

When a Santa Ana blows fire down the coast
do you run to meet it in a leisure suit
or with a silicon chip?

Does a squirrel stash nuts
of self-pity up its ass?

What are verses for?

And the raisin-light dribbling
in the clerestory faded,
and it was cold

as I backed down the aisle:

"We'll talk more when you're off duty."

A Letter to Wallace Stevens

1

After the Reformation had settled the loamy soil
and the lettuce-green fields of dollars,
the clouds drifted away, and light fell everywhere.
Even the snow bloomed and New Hampshire was a big peony.

A red barn shone on a hill
with scattered hemlocks and white pines
and the gates of all the picket fences were big shut-eyes.

2

Sometime after the Civil War, the bronze wing of liberty
took off like the ribboning smoke of a Frick factory,
and all the citizens in towns from Stockbridge to Willamette
ran wild on the 4th. The sound of piccolos lingered,
and the shiny nickel of the sun stood still before it
fizzed in the windshield of a Ford.
By then you were a lawyer.

3

Charles Ives was a bandmaster in Danbury, and you didn't
give him the time of day. He played shortstop on the piano.
He never made it to his tonic home base, and his half-tones
were like oak leaves slapping clapboard.

4

How Miltonic are we anyway?

5

In that red glass of the imagination,
in that tingling crystal of the chandelier
where light freezes in its own prism

and the apogee of the green lawns of New Haven
wane like Persian carpets in twilight,
there you saw a pitcher, perhaps from Delft,
next to a plate of mangoes.

6

But still, history is a boomerang,
and the aborigines never threw one without a shield.

7

Beyond the porches of Key West, beyond the bougainvillea,
your speech skipped on tepid waves,
was lapped and lapped by lovers and friends,
by scholars who loved romantic nights of the sun.

But the fruits and pendants, the colorful cloth,
the dry palm fronds, and the fake voodoo wood
Cortés brought back as souvenirs
were just souvenirs. And the shacks and the cane and the
hacked plantain were tableaux,
and who saw them from your dark shore?

8

The Protestant dinner plate is a segregated place,
where the steak hardens, and the peas
sit frightened in their corner while mashed potatoes ossify.
Some gin and ice cream, and the terror of loneliness
goes for a while.

9

As they say in the sunny climes,
un abrazo.

After the Survivors Are Gone

I tried to imagine the Vilna ghetto,
to see a persimmon tree after the flash at Nagasaki.
Because my own tree had been hacked,
I tried to kiss the lips of Armenia.

At the table and the altar
we said some words written ages ago.
Have we settled for just the wine and bread,
for candles lit and snuffed?

Let us remember how the law has failed us.
Let us remember the child naked,
waiting to be shot on a bright day
with tulips blooming around the ditch.

We shall not forget the earth,
the artifact, the particular song,
the dirt of an idiom—
things that stick in the ear.

Ocean

Out of her salt hips
poured my umbel.

My mouth full of shells
and her tongue
a lemon bristling my teeth.

Foam flowered
and the black grapes
tasted sweet again.

I smelled fenugreek,
the cherry pit's talcum,
cod drying like a sandy slipper.

An amaryllis opened
in my throat,

and the pain issued
toward the islands.

FROM *REPLY FROM*
WILDERNESS ISLAND
(1988)

The Creases

Over the foothills of the Chenango Valley
the evening air comes over clumps of swamp pine

and a tractor almost invisible in hay.
The creases the shadows make

on the trees and farmland send
the cold mist of the faraway coast.

Now the dead seem all alike—
they used to be my friends, they told me secrets.

With ocean breaking over my wrists,
I feel the dead too feel shame

and they must withhold just
as once they dished it out.

The voices of my father and his father grow softer
and if I can't understand them . . .

my brain folded in its clam-like
way can piss out the brine

(for there's brine that cures peppers and goat's cheese
and salt that makes terror in us all).

The ocean runnels up
the involuted imprints in the sand left by the living.

The sky's blues and grays join
to make creases for the lips of the dead.

Swamp pines recede
and the foothills fold into my house.

Night Blue Fishing on Block Island

Water funnels my ankles
   warmer than the air
and sucks away so I see

only scudding white
   pour out of itself
five feet from my half-dead flashlight

like snakes splitting apart
   in the sleazy air.
I cast several times and there's nothing,

and the water rises higher.
   My shins in the world's solution
the rest of me chilling in the wind—

until I get a yank and feel
   the metal sink and jilt
till it's busted through a gill

and I move farther out
   to tire him out
and the tide rises up my cock.

From the corner of my eye
   I see a parabolic arc
something winging out next to me,

I keep giving line to the blue,
   the current pressing my knees
waves slapping my thighs

and I think 9 pounds or more
    a bloated eye
and the water streaked with blood—

A cloud passes and moonlight falls
   in several shafts on the black
and I recognize his side-face,

though he takes no notice of me,
   and fishes steadily.
The wind between us is too loud.

He balances the line on his index finger
   (I recognize his patience)
and his whole side-face is silver.

I start to pull my own slack back.
   He's giving in,
and I think of a lashed body

swerving in the black waves.
   I'm cold and sweating in the salt;
another cloud cuts off half the moon.

His silver arms are gone,
   and there is only wind coming
from the place where I saw his side-face.

I look hard and the ocean
   is a wide place before me,
as I back through the folds of algae

and bring the fish up, three hooks
   in his mouth.
He's dead. 4 months my father's dead.

I throw the fish, 5 pounds
    or so, in a plastic cooler
hooked and bleeding; barely breathing.

I start the car
    my legs warmed by the seat.
A bluefish in a cooler steaming.

I gut him in the garage
    so I won't wake anybody;
throw the head to the cats.

Thoreau at Nauset

I watched the kelp in particular,
spread on the sand
like some homespun.

Earweed, tangle, devil's-
apron, sole-leather, ribbon weed;
it's a con artist.

Umbilical in the bubbles.
Unsnarled by the tide.

When it catches the sun,
it's a budding anemone.

I took the first chance
to whittle some up.

It could've been sea-otter's-cabbage,
which can hit a hundred feet.

Strange wide softness.
Root-like holdfast.
I cut the stipe.

Felt its rubber.
Pulled apart branching stalks
and wrapped the blades'

still puffing bladders
around my wrists.

Then sun spilled like gilt
on onionskin.

With a match and small twigs
I made a small fire
to cook my clam.

Tough and sweet.
A little water and some bread,
and I'd have called it a feast.

*

Sat at the Charity House
till dusk.

No windows or sliding shutters.

I knelt by a knothole in the door.
Cold air moved through the straw-
stuffed clapboards.

My eye drifted in the quiet dark.
The floor was breathing.
I stood there light as hay

dilating

my skin—a man-o'-war's
after a sculler slits it
and the ink spills out.

for Hyatt and Louise Waggoner

To Arshile Gorky

1

The sun hangs all day like summer
on my back. Chestnut leaves are fan-tails.
A rose against the hemlock is purple air.
Hummingbirds plume the fuchsia.

2

When I was a kid we had a garden
hanging with heavy things. Eggplants
almost black made shell scars in the mud.
Peppers and zucchini dragged along the furrows.
My mother pickled every cuke in the piss-colored
vinegar jars crammed with dill.
Ivy, moss, and grass were silver light at dusk.

3

The suckle falls like white water
on the side fence. In the wild-carrot
eggs are eyes; rabbits are knot-holes.
Tendrils loop like cut zither strings.
A raccoon hides in my stomach.
In the morning the milkweed comes.

4

Your mother is dried fruit in a dish.
Columbine is a flock of doves taking off.

5

Between a lake in Armenia and
my suburban house,
you're lamb bones in the ground—
chalk rising in the morning air.

Camille Claudel, Some Notes

1

No restraint. No faith.

Pollaiuolo's balls were the Louvre.

The studio stank of us.
I wasn't his muse or his equal.

2

Flayed arms on an Etruscan bowl
dim gutter light in the apse—
clerestory sun.

We loved ourselves in gouged sockets.

Amiens.

3

I showed him Balzac's cloak.
I pulled him from the slate and weeds of Normandy.
My father would've fed him with the dogs.

4

He felt that scream of Ugolino's
as if he had swallowed my hand.

In that cell where we worked
fungus and moss grew,
the iron sink stank like rotting organs.
Among wet rags, cigarette ashes, broken wood, and calipers
I found Dante.

5

On sunny days he thought he was Fra Filippo.
Crap. The sky is one blank cloud; the firmament
just marl. I told him the bowels are the bowels
not the seat of pity.
The cunt, the cunt—no eternal tunnel.

6

The Burghers of Calais. That was us.
Not those busts he did of me or *The Kiss.*
Too smooth. For the sitting rooms
of the petite bourgeoisie. *Calais:* hungering faces
and the body's planes moving in light,
the necks of dying lucid minds.

I furrowed the torso of the burgher on the right—
plowed my love into his ribs, held each thorny toe
welded to the blood and glass of history.
I licked his ass to taste his fear—
smelled the bronze in my own piss.

7

He effaced me beneath the skylight,
the air between us flushed.

That night I read Baudelaire to him out loud,
he crawled in me like a frightened dog.

8

I smell trees. Fleshy stems, like lilypads
in June at Renoir's when the rank white cups opened
and the mud was warm between us.

The nurses in their cheesecloth suits stare
at me like chimps in cages.
In the aviary that summer birds called like the

blue-sky-kingfisher

9

The fields fill up—
sifted flour   white wind   downy wings

the halo of alabaster rising in the right
panel of Grünewald's Altarpiece

it falls and falls

the holes in the barn roof a torso of an upturned oak
armatures of apple trees rock and shinbones
a twisted birch pulled out of itself
the hammered mud of horses

10

My shawl's rose-tinged
so is the air in sleep
like his head

I smashed in March
and the dust came down
on the concourse and carriages.

Pigeons went up too
like eye-sockets of the Antichrist.

Poppies

1

Bright orange in the morning
cupping the fragrant air
of the upstate summer.

All my aunt remembered of Armenia.

In the hot sun,
I look them dead center—
orange paper streaked black;

pollen gets in my nose.

When I look into the pit,
the base of the pistil's missing.

2

When the buttery light of the moon
falls on them,

I see into their eyes.

Men and women who bore my name
have gone from face to bone

with the quickness that night
has made the poppies
into nothing.

3

Not only for Armenia
do these poppies give up their petals.

4

Off long stems black eyes sway
in the morning wind.

The anther sacs are busted—
filaments rise past my window.

Parts of Peonies

It rained so much in June
some grew to look like stuffed cabbage
or the small heads of lambs.

Even the stigmas were buried
in the dense red and white.

All day I tried to put
my hands into their swollen insides.
I thought my touch would reawaken.

In the slightest breeze
they swooned
and things fell out—

(their nectar glands
sweet and white on my hands)

a goat's spongy sac,
the shard of a wooden belfry,
a peeling eucalyptus,

and here in my small upstate garden,
a bladder and a nest are the same,

a bird drops eggs everywhere.

I close my eyes in the harsh light,
and the black spots become peonies.

for Terrence Des Pres

Domestic Lament

1

Like heavy muslin
there's air around my house.
A goblet half-full
of vinegar on my desk.

Tangerines are open globes
in a bowl.

I keep looking
as if I were thinking on the fog
settling into the orchards,
thinking of what's beyond me.

Downstairs, oil in a skillet—
garlic browns
as if from another year

as from a time
when you were a shape in my life.

The pots hanging over the sink
are from some other kitchen
where I once lived.

2

I look into the vaporous evening
making a lap
between two hills.

When certain shadows dovetail
and make a spectacular shadow
in a corner of the house
you keep me from myself.

Outside, there you are

eyelashes on a bird's nest
a graceful branch like a clavicle,
toenails, elongated fingers
sprouting from the upturned roots of an apple tree.

Whole trees splinter inside me.

3

You sleep somewhere
beyond the white air.

Your heart's a plucking syllable,
a space like some unfathomable
vertebra—

4

Outside, the street's not visible.

When you turn over,
the water breaks on the air
between us.

A Version of Paolo and Francesca

Paolo

It was not Virgil you read
(though I asked you to), but the Peruvian,
part Indian, part cousin of Lorca

whose words were spiky points,
wafts of privet, week-old cod.

When you breathed them at me
nothing in the outer world ceased
its turbulent grim direction.

You breathed on my unhooked
eyes and uncovered me.

Above the roof a windfucker smacked
the air,
and wind kept eating the island rocks.

Francesca

We ate along the riverside at sundown.
The clear green juice dripped from my mouth.

We didn't fuck missionary on clean sheets.
I lost my head between your legs.
My nose spreading like honey.

A whiff of narcissus swept across us.
I ate the flowers whole, tried to outfox
Satan with my tongue.

I felt as if I shimmied up your legs to find
this point on the Jersey cliffs.
The sun was God's eye.

I plugged my ears so I wouldn't hear your crappy verse,
then tore into your pants like a scared cat.

The Chrysler Building was a pin.
I tasted you five hundred feet
as the Hudson pulled me under.

I Wish Us Back to Mud

I wish us back to mud
as November light
falls on the rotting wood
and vines in piles by the shed.

May we resolve what we can't
say in the night when we lie
together without reason
and can't receive the grace

we imagine on the hills.
I wish us back to mud
for scouring rush and blue-
eyed grass have gone before us.

May we know the color
of our blood is mud
and that we're inevitable
as chicory and wild carrot.

I wish us back to mud
for love that asks us
to be free of nothing
and nothing to be free of us.

Blood Pudding, Antigua, W.I.
(Helen, eight months pregnant)

1

The woman told me her father
held the pig firm by the ass
and her mother slit its throat

so the cranberry blood spilled
into a bowl.

When the shit was cleaned
from the stomach,
the fibrous lining
bristling with veins,

her mother sewed one end shut
with catgut.

The rice steamed and seasoned
in the family way:
the onion almost invisible—
pepper, clove, allspice;
then into the bowl to soak

and into the empty stomach,
the other end folded down;
the whole bag of blood
plunged into noisy boiling water.

2

Out of gurgle and salt.
Up from stinking chicken gizzards

broken hog knuckles
hanging goat lung, trachea,
epiglottis, rancid tonsil bulbs.

From the whirling pool of camel jaws,
toothless and hungry—
the sheep tongues' Ancient Days
dragging their red sheaths
across the sand.

Out of dog nostrils quivering in wet death—
down from tendrilous mucus
spun from a calm-sea membrane.

Into the raucous flush
of cartilage and hair and the septum
dividing dark and light.

Out from the one nose
which blew into dust

so the wet shape of being
could rise into the voiceless night

before it could walk toward
Canaan in gumless joy and material lust

and the screeching wind
of its own throat.

3

From the beach café
we watch the moon
rising over the Caribbean.

Our son or daughter stretches you now,
moving toward your lungs,
pushing to the sternum
where the higher air circulates.

The blood pudding in its quarter-moon sac
steams in the night air—
thick brown with platelets

as we break the lining with our forks
solid, liquid, gas:
pig blood rising from its casing
into circles

rings of air inside
rings of air.

Fish Mouth

In late August I come back
to the Sound for blues and fluke.
I wait with patience beneath
this copper sky; an oil slick
refracts the morning light.

I pull a fish, a good four-pound
fluke and catch my hand on the barb.
A three-inch gash bleeds
down my wrist; the salty flounder
burns into my skin.

His eyes are flat and glassy in the air.
My vision too is going bad.
I try to stop the bleeding with a cloth
which turns, in a minute,
dark as fish liver.

I feel the scar along my head
you stitched when I was ten.
A father in the sweaty night
tying up his son's skin.

I lay an hour while you
tweezed and cut black thread.
Stitched, clipped, pulled
the cells tight.

A bass was swimming in me then,
a blue-black scaly thing
turning in the tangle of myself,
I hardly knew.

Now, I'm alone in this small boat,
a salty cut I try to bind with a rag.
It's open like a fish mouth.
The fluke is drying on the floor,
I should throw it back.

There's an imprint of scissored
teeth bound into my head
like fins that turn behind my eyes.

A Country House

The moon glares across
an open field and there's

a lump of deer guts
like a shapeless sculpture.
The air keeps cutting
at the corn stubble I can't see.

I was in the eaves
and found I couldn't stay.
The beams are simple timbers
made of simple trees.

The wind on the house
breaks some shingles loose,
and I want a deer to rise
from the pile of himself.

I'm a man in a country house.
Flanks and splints of oak are all
that keep the night off my back.
Outside, the ground turns

harder than a skull,
and some deer walk
into the eyeholes of the night.
A son must face a treeless place,

a country house held up
by trunks and branches older than man.

Things out there are still.
My father doesn't walk upon the earth.

Mussel Shell

I must come when the sky is burnt
the color of a mussel shell—
my head bloated as the stomach of a clam,
my hands wet as gills—

to see each furled pocket the wind makes
on the bay as a simple pearl-like
scale on the drying side of a bass.

How many scales, then, make this inlet?
How many inlets make the water,
or cups of light unfurl in just a minute of wind?

I have to let my net stay in a lump on the dock;
give up my tackle, throw the squid heads back,
let the night crawlers loose in the earth;
my tangled lines must pass over the school
of fluke that comes with evening sun.

I must sit and wait with nothing but my eyes—
my skin flaking day by day,
salt eating down my neck.

I have to come and learn to stutter once again
while all around me empty clams
are taking in and letting go

their viscid selves that wane
and bloat for ages
until they are something not one of us can see.

Jersey Bait Shack

If I can find this place near-abandoned
in early fall with its weather-bitten shingles
still the grainy color of ash and its roof
warping from the spray,
the only window boarded up

where there is a secret side door
that now in September unswells,
and if I work the latch just right
I'll find the dark calm inner air
growing toward my face.

Into a room where barrels—once
filled with clams, chubs, crab-ends,
the scum of minnows and night crawlers,
and squid-bits—are dark holes reeking,
and I'm on my hands and knees

in the stink of aftermath,
and all this shit that could've
been gold—to hook
the ghostly thing that glides
down there in some adoring tide—

is absence—and is telling me
how long I have to soak beneath the bait.

FROM *SAD DAYS*
OF LIGHT
(1983)

The History of Armenia

Last night
my grandmother returned
in her brown dress
standing on Oraton Parkway
where we used to walk
and watch the highway
being dug out.
She stood against
a backdrop of steam hammers
and bulldozers,
a bag of fruit
in her hand,
the wind blowing
through her eyes.

I was running
toward her
in a drizzle
with the morning paper.
When I told her
I was hungry, she said,
in the grocery store
a man is standing
to his ankles in blood,
the babies in East Orange
have disappeared,
maybe eaten
by the machinery
on this long road.

When I asked for my mother
she said, gone,
all gone.

The girls went for soda,
maybe the Coke was bad,
the candy sour.
This morning the beds
are empty, water off,
toilets dry.
When I went to the garden
for squash
only stump was there.
When I went to clip
parsley
only a hole.

We walked past piles
of gray cinder and cement
trucks; there were no men.
She said Grandpa left
in the morning,
in the dark;
he had pants to press
for the firemen of
East Orange.
They called him
in the middle of night,
West Orange was burning,
Bloomfield and Newark
were gone.

One woman carried
the arms of her child
to East Orange last night
and fell on her uncle's
stoop, two boys came
with the skin
of their legs
in their pockets
and turned themselves in

to local officials;
this morning sun
is red and spreading.

If I go to sleep
tonight, she said,
the ceiling will open
and bodies will fall
from clouds. *Yavrey,*
where is the angel
without sword, *Yavrey,*
where is the angel
without six fingers
and a missing leg,
the angel with news
the water will be clear
and have fish.

Grandpa is pressing pants.
They came for him
before the birds were up—
he left without shoes
or tie, shirt or suspenders.
It was quiet.
The birds, the birds
were still sleeping.

Road to Aleppo, 1915

A flame like a leaf eaten
in the sun followed you—
a white light rose higher
than the mountain,
and singed the corner of your eye
when you turned to find
the screaming trees
dissolving to the plain.

Even when the sun dropped,
the ground was heat and bayonets,
and in the Turkish wind
the throats of boys
kept ringing in your ears.

Your breath like horizon
settled into black.
You stuttered every mile
to your daughters'
shorter steps.

The air, almost gone,
filled inside your dress.

Post-Traumatic Shock, Newark,
New Jersey, 1942

Shirts hang in the glass showcase
behind the gold *French Cleaners,*

when I open the door,
naphthalene rises
into the no-legs.

Delphiniums are blue like
the decanters of cologne from Paris.
That's my brother's house.

God's face on a wooden belfry.
God's lips. God's nose.
God's innocent little prick.

At the butcher's those are cow's eyes
with the visionary gleam of things
in the dead sand.

I'm the star of a Jew
rising from the beery foam
of Chaplin's moustache.

It was a dirt road
like the head of an elk
or these hanging ribs.

Figs at Delaney's all
the way from Smyrna
like shit in cellophane.

On the road. We were going there,
and then Hawaii turned into white light
on the screen of the Philco.

Kamikaze metal.
A runway of gin and broken glass.
Naphthalene of the Red Cross nurses.

Yes, yes, the child's mine.
No Armenians left?

Jimmy Stewart you bastard
I'm here with some shopping bags.

The Claim

APPLICATION FOR THE SUPPORT OF
    CLAIMS AGAINST FOREIGN GOVERNMENTS

    May 15, 1919, Department of State

Light perfumed wind
off the Park, the chestnuts arched
over Fifth Avenue.
I'm the age she was in 1915.

Q.1. Give the (a) name, (b) residence, and (c) occupation
A.1. (a) Nafina Hagop Chilinguirian (born Shekerlemedjian)
(b) Ghuri St., Aleppo, Syria (c) Tailoress.

A.2. (a) complete ownership (b) since August 1915
(c) From my husband Hagop Chilinguirian, the
original claimant who was a citizen of U.S.A.
beginning his minority till the year 1909 A.D. when

History is a man's breath.
Whatever I take in I give out,
mother of my mother

her wobbly skeletal frame,
the high-pitched calcium
    of the bones
in the air I breathe

my head feathery
in the hot June wind.

he returned in order to arrange his affairs but he
died during our deportation

My grandmother used to say:
they went there—
they were going
to the river Tigris.

—family who are perished on account of the deportation
leaving me and my brother Thomas Shekerlemedjian
now residing at
U.S.A.
Box 125 West Hoboken, New Jersey

(Answer Question 15 c)

I, Lucia Der Hovsepian, 45 years old, born in Diarbekir
Turkey, residing in Zeki st., Aleppo, Syria, occupying
by domestic works residing before the deportation in
Diarbekir, do solemnly affirm that Nafina Hagop Chilinguirian
had her birth certificate

all over Central Park today   hydrangea opening

but it was lost during the deportation;
that she is born in Diarbekir, Turkey, at 22nd October 1890
of the parents Hagop Shekerlemedjian and Lucia Nadjarian

who deprived me of my ripe years? who?
I heard her say this once behind closed doors

but when I walked into
the room no one else was there
Walls. No moldings. Floating prayer rugs
flowers on sand/   running vines/   a medallion   swinging in the wind

(A) GENERAL QUESTIONS

14. State race to which claimant belongs—
    Armenian, white

22 October 1890 Diarbekir, Turkey
my birth certificate was lost
attached the affidavit for

She filed the claim after she arrived in New Jersey—
A law firm in Newark—right through to the State Dept.
my aunt said; nothing happened
for sixty years in the third drawer of the dresser

I, Père Harutiun Yessayan, the Prelate of Armenians
in Aleppo . . . do hereby certify that I have no
interest in the claim
        PRELATURE   ALEP   1919

On this steamy island
I smell the oil rags of women

We the undersigned of this affidavit
do solemnly affirm that Hagop Chilinguirian
        the husband of Nafina
is of the U.S.A.

I used to roll grape leaves
with her Sunday after church
we washed off the brine
cut the thick part of the stem out

SECTION V
        FACTS REGARDING CLAIM

Q.55. Give an itemized statement of property entirely lost
description of damage   value in dollars American   losses

2500 kg. of sugar a 3 p. gold	750 Ltq.
household furniture	250
goods left at my husband's shop	
1000 kg. of sugar	500

5000 kg. of coffee a 15 p. gold	750
2000 kg. of hemp-cords	100
1000 parcels of sacks	250
1000 curry combs a 5 p. gold	750
25,000 kg. of rice	750
6000 kg. of gall-nut	100

spice mountain
spice mountain

the nose becomes powder
the hair dust

Ready money robbed on the way by the Turks
the money necessary to rear my two daughters,
Gladys 7 years old and Alice 5 years old,
till their marriage   2000

Carrion of a soup
coppery urine on my fingers;

      horse screams   go back
       curry combs   mane   meat stink

my grandmother's voice
reverberations off the walls
walls where nations disappear
the walls around Diarbekir
walls around   around
walls   a trellis of grapes

TOTAL IN GOLD   5900 Ltq.
in American dollars at the rate of 1915 A.D. 68,750 dollars

The aphrodisiac privet along the Park

the ripe years   a bowl of pears
a sack of peaches   a body

list of the losses and injuries come down
by inheritance from our relatives indicated below

My brother Harutiun Shekerlemedjian, merchant
had at Karadja Hagh, a village in Diarbekir,
150 tons of rice kept in three wells   captured
by the government   3500 Ltq.   in his shop at the market-
place goods: calicoes, clothes, silken clothes
        at the shop at Iz-ed-din:
cotton-clothes, calicoes, leathers

500 sheep   village Talavi   150 tons of rice in three wells
jewels and money kept under the ground in a box

The blood value for a person was ordered to be 350 Ltq.
        by decree of the Sultan

I feel the jackal
in my pants

My sister Hadji Anna captured by a Turk named Hadji Bakkar

        take nothing   house
        burning   horse-flame

C) My father Hagop Shekerlemedjian, 75 years old,
    killed by Turks

My mother Lucia Shekerlemedjian, 50 years old,
    killed by Turks   350
My brother Dikran Shekerlemedjian, 35 years old,
    killed by Turks   350
His son Karnig Shekerlemedjian   7 years old
    killed by Turks   350

        this is good for you, she said,
        the olive oil virgin
        the leaves baby green

His son Diran Shekerlemedjian, 4 years old
    killed by Turks   350
My brother Harutiun Shekerlemedjian, 30 years old
    killed by Turks   350
His son Levon Shekerlemedjian, 2 years old
    killed by Turks   350
His daughter Azniv Shekerlemedjian, 5 years old
    killed by Turks   350
My sister Hadji Anna Derhovsepian, 28 years old
    killed by Turks   350
My sister Arusyag Berberian, 25 years old
    killed by Turks   350

> *By the lofty cedars of Lebanon*
> *and the oaks of Bashan*
> *there I used to lie*
> *when I was a girl*

We the undersigned of this affidavit, Thomas Alchikian, 50
years old, Armenian shoemaker, and Yervant Ekmekdjian, 35,
Armenian blacksmith, solemnly affirm that Nafina Hagop
    Chilinguirian
is the very owner

lamb-tongue   cow-foot   human eye

The tulips are blinding
along 64th Street

My husband in spite of that he was a citizen of U.S.A.
was forced . . . as he was feeble and indisposed being subjected to

    such conditions
    and seeing our relatives killed
    inhumanly, he could not support the life

    leaving me a widow with my two orphan daughters
    Gladys 7 and Alice 5

We the remaining deportees, women and children
were forced to walk without being allowed even
to buy some bread to eat. Frequently we were
robbed by Turks as if they would carry us safely
to our destiny which was entirely unknown

So for thirty days we were obliged to wander
through mountains and valleys   fatigue and hunger
enforced by the whip of the gendarmes diminished
the number of deportees

> *my brothers' heads are*
> *on the vine, on the vine;*
> *what rots is in the pot*

After many dangers whose description would take
much time a few women and children included I myself
arrived at Aleppo Syria beginning September 1915

that the Turk people plundered and captured
    that they are all killed by the Turks
        during our deportation

a peak where Noah landed
        dove come back
        with a twig

QUESTION 63

1 August 1915 our parish in Diarbekir was besieged by the gendarmes
. . . the same day with the menace of death
they removed us, the Armenians

> *red unguent crow-beak   anise*
> *leave by the stable   the lake is fire*

the Turk people plundered and captured our goods   the deporter
gendarmes separated the men from the women
and binding them to each other,
they carried all of us to an unknown direction

Sunday her coat like incense

After three days, they killed one by one the man deportees
of whom only a few were saved. So were killed mercilessly my
brothers and sisters and

> *in Armenian we do not say*
> *for ever and ever, Amen.*
> *It means unto the Ages of Ages.*

Since then I am supported by the Hon. Consulate
of U.S.A. at Aleppo

I remember when
she helped me blow
the candles out,
my fifth birthday;
no light, only curls
of smoke in the kitchen.

The deportation and the fiendish steps taken
against the Armenians in general being well
known by the civilized world, I do not mention
other evidences concerning this matter
    Only
       I assert that:

> *how long will they cook   the eyes   the eyes of men*
> *where is the Black Sea   is the sea Black?*
> *why do women wear black to church?*

I am a human being . . . it was impossible to
have by me the documentary evidence concerning my
losses but my co-deportees saved from death
witness that
                    I am
I am human   herewith affidavit.

Granny, Making Soup

In its stone pores
this pot holds
what's left of time—

early mint, dill, walnut-root,
the dust of the rusty stick of cinnamon
we pass from generation
to generation;

run your finger along
the curve, it's soft
like a fine shell,
smell the bottom,
it's stronger
than when my grandmother
rubbed it with her palm.

*

I break the shoulder bones
apart, no knife, nothing metal—
the white ball of the joint
we'll all chew later.
Now, the socket
from which it is pulled
is the empty round
where we join.

I hacked three times a week
a lamb like this
for market—

and I knew when
their blue throats

swallowed in my hand,
how close we were to soup,
and when the pink-gray skin,
shaved and glowing
in the sun
was slit and wheezing
and crying out its guts,
I took a fingerful
of blood.

*

Here, the white string
the teeth can't cut
must be left.

You must take the tendon
and give it to the water
of the soup.

When I see it
in the cauldron
like a frazzled strand of fish,
I think how like
the body fiber
is the ankle of a goat
who wanders
on the dry steppe
for weeks and weeks
till from some small cave
there is water
thin and clear singing
along the sand

and we drink
we all drink.

*

When the water rises
in this pot
and a slow steam comes
over the clean bones
and shoulder fat,
there's a low gurgle
and the marrow moves.
The flecks of basil open
like small leaves
and the celery grows dark,
bends its head
for bottom.

I've watched this, Peter,
in the black
of the cauldron
when there was no light—
a first steam started.
I could hear the grain
in my spoon settle
and my hair tightened
as in August
on the wharf.

In an hour the girls
will sneak in to taste,
Grandpa will loosen his tie,
the plants will droop,

but for now
it's all at bottom.

★

Always in afternoon
you let the pot alone

the water will take
from the bones
what the lamb takes from the earth,

the water will take
from the marrow
what the lamb's mouth
takes from the low hills:
some high grass
beyond the wet meadow
and the weeds around
the eucalyptus
and in night
when the lamb takes
the fig and breaks it open
so the seed covers ground—

this too
the water takes
from the bones.

And when the lamb
wanders beyond the steppe
to the first ledge
of the mountain
and the wildcat pins
him to the dust
and dry red shale,
and tears him
almost woolless
until the bleat
of his throat is hushed,
and his organs are gnashed
to nothing,
and he is open
and clean of everything

but the long bones
of his back
thinner than the cat's teeth,
and the blood
dries on the skin
and the feathers
of gray wool are left
for the birds—

this too
the water takes
from the bones.

*

And when we return
in evening,
the water will be full
of the stone
and like a voice
it will moan
with its tendon, fat, and bone,
and with the little meat
we've left for our own teeth,

and then, Peter,
we'll have broth—

and when you
take it to your lips
you'll take it
all in.

Three Museum Offerings
(Native American Artifacts
at the Whitney)

1

The pain is in the grain of wood.
The feet twist where the root was pulled
from the ground.
A crown of thorns from brier ruddled
and twined around the head.

In certain towns of the Southwest
a woman dressed as death
danced for three days
before falling to her knees
at the foot of this cross.

★

Accept the rib I remove from his chest.
They stirred red ocher with it
to paint the woman's bones,
then returned it to its place.

2

This wooden mask
kept winter out of the Eskimos' blood.
The hue of green around the eyes
kept the face from disappearing into snow.

When a woman came to the shaman
with her sick child,
he stalked the tundra for twenty days
and wandered out over hard water.

When he returned with fish ovaries
seals reappeared and the Kuskokwim broke open.

★

Accept this shell that covered
his cheekbone and this piece of mouth
blushed and open.

3

This spear weathered and white was used
by Indians of the Plains to cut and drain.
It bled bad dreams, delirium, and ghosts.

When a mother came from her sleep in fever,
two infants strapped to her legs,
the skin of her parents—ash;
a medicine man slit her arm
and drank blood.

★

Accept this bone handle worn and smooth
and this chip of slate.
It still cuts skin.

for my mother and Aunt Lucille

That Is Why This Day Passes
Like a Thousand Lilies

There are whole days of light
that are sad,
there are high trees on the far slope
and small beds of lilies
that give back the day
and make the windows tremble.
There is an outline to the hills
that aches like a woman's body,

and there are gullies on the slopes
I cannot see,
small water for the trees
to sink in.

That is why this day passes
like a thousand lilies
and why I stay inside and breathe
too fast.

Outside the pavement smells
of small flowers and petroleum.
The moss shines on spiders and ants.
There's a quiet to the alley trailing
off to the fat woman shouting at her dog,
and for that I stay inside
and listen to the floorboards.

It is not just the light passing
that makes the cows sound far and heavy
and moves me from corner to corner of this room
beckoning me to shout at the onions on the shelf
and laugh at the tomatoes growing old on the sill

but the way the nearest hills
go darker than the trees they lose
and the flax drones around
the ankles of the farmers,
that leaves my heart shouting at my chest
and my veins weeping
for the trees they never hear

that keeps me with the cupboards full of cans
and dishes, and the long squashes
by the window going soft,
that keeps me here standing over my empty shoes.

The Rise in the Night

It should be warm tonight
but a chill comes up
from the ground through my legs
and my hands are like dead flowers
with the last color leaving.

All the houses are low and far away
and if there is a light on
I cannot tell it from the gray cat,

and if there were voices at my back
when the sky was rosy
they've given way to the chattering leaves
and the miles of slow-turning worms.

All week it has rained
and it has rained so much
I began to feel how full of water
the dead must be.
I began to feel with my eyes
and they told me when the cold
breaks like an ocean
the ground is two lips that part
and everything crawls out.

Tonight this field is drying
and everything is dying back
everything is an open nerve

and I can hear—
the snakes breathing through the green
the chinks and bulbs hissing in their husks

the vines, the ones that crawl and you never see,
are bleeding from the air.

And there's a low snoring
that's more than wind,
a low snoring from my father
in his dark bed
making a gust with his parting nose
beneath a pile of blossoms and bark,
and there is a prowling snout
rising up through my legs,
raising its head into my chest,
and I hear—

because it has stopped raining
and I hear my ears breathing
and the trees settling into their wood,
this Beast with its hair makes
a sound I know,

and it will find its two legs
and carry a ton of mud
with roots and eggs and shiny beetles,
and it will carry the legs of my cousins
and my grandmother's shoes—

it will rise with my father's veins
and the iridescent stones
and the eyes of squirrels clear as water—

Seferis Returning to Smyrna, 1950

A thread of shore
is whiter than the sky.
Fishing boats cast no shadows
and the lighthouse stands,
a cylinder of salt.

The street you take is shrunken
and your legs are numb
as if the merchant selling fruit
recognized your eyes.

Past the courtyard of St. Nicholas
now remade into a school,
almond trees are stumps.
Flaming pomegranates you snaked
through to catch the night barge
to Marseilles are now light
stains beneath your feet.

In your grandmother's garden
where the widows sat
to watch the light fall
on the silent harbor,
the trellis draped with grapes
returns a scent
of your brother's shirt.

Where the votive rags
hung on the fig trees,
there's a stink of smoking
fruit like a hole
in a high blue sky.

All evening you walk hot streets,
loukoumades rising sweet
in your nose and hollow villas
falling where a man
like your uncle rummages.

A harbor of skin and wind
sends back a breath
and the lighthouse loses shape
against the sky.

For My Grandmother,
Coming Back

For the dusty rugs
and the dye of blue-roots,
for the pale red stomachs of sheep,
you come back.

For the brass ladle
and the porous pot of black
from your dinner of fires,
I call your name like a bird.

For the purple fruit
for the carrots like cut fingers
for the riverbed damp with flesh,
you come back.

For the field of goats
wet and gray,
for the hooves and sharp bones
floating in the broth,
I wave my arms full of wind.

For the tumbling barrel
of red peppers,
for the milled mountain of wheat,
for the broken necks
of squash fat and full of seed,
I let my throat open.

For the lips of young boys
bitten through,
for the eyes of virgins brown
and bleating on the hill,

for the petticoat of your daughter
shivering by the lake,
for the yarn of her arms
unwinding at her father's last shout.

For the lamb punctured
from the raw opening
to his red teeth,
for the lamb rotating
like the sun
on its spit,
for the eyes that fall
into the fire,
for the tongue tender and full,
for the lungs smoldering
like leaves
and the breasts spilling
like yellow milk
and the stomach heaving
its fistful of days
like red water falling
into the stream,

I wave my arms full of birds
full of dry gusts
full of burning clothes,
and you come back,
you come back.

FROM *FATHER FISHEYE*
(1979)

After We Split

I drove back and there were still
green veins in the leaves.

I mulched the new hemlocks,
cut back the suckle.
It was shrill without you and the cicadas.

I backed down a dirt road,
and a thin line of color above the mountains
wavered in the rearview mirror of the station wagon
which was crammed with the privet we breathed all summer,

and a dogwood August turned to brush,
tomatoes—green, orange, yellow-mold,
hanging on frost-scalded vines
and sacked in wet newspapers like dead arteries,

also bushes of Tropicanas, beetle-chewed,
gummed with white powder—
stiff as pricks.

I unlatched the tailgate,
and the hinges croaked.
I yanked till it all spilled out,

then flicked a match
and the first smoke smoldered,
a cringe of blue cracked and spread like a wave

till there was a white flame
showing the trees big as they are,
shaking on the mountain.

Winter Revival

Trees make light seem possible,
black, gray, then teal.

A frozen wing of something, and the snow's there.
On the gutter pipe the ivy's frozen fragile as a cannula.

I can see a cellophane Christmas tree in the manager's office
blinking in a car window.

I could send Latin words to you,
past the blue molecules of the wren.

I'd tell you I memorized them from a painting
by a Flemish master and that on the scroll
behind the Lamb they were drawn like silk.

Now, I'm the skin of a lizard.
My tongue's vermicular afloat,

I'd tell you that this morning
even the apple in the Madonna's hand would harden.

The Christmas tree keeps flashing
and the fovea shrinks like a glazed shrub.

Outside there's a blinking yellow traffic light
and a general store.

Eggs freeze in the ovaries of a hen.

A Sequence of Wind Between Seasons

40 and
oaks crack.

Ground loosens.
Tendons make dents

in the riverbank.
Things rise from the bottom,

and the face is after-image.
Some jays eat mud.

Even weasels lose their fur.
Holes thaw like silence.

Twigs float in the mouth.
The eyes see eggs.

The body is where
a thousand swallows land.

Nests aren't abandoned—
A nose distills stones.

A river turns black
like a crow in glare.

Graham House, April '76

In a late REM cycle I caught something,
and the same man rode in the heat on an ass.
The TV went horizontal. Darts caught the ten-
point rim. On the jukebox a cover of "Tutti Frutti";
some Bantu trekking north for water;
the newsprint's white and smooth and bright.

When I wake, the gutters are spiles
of ice, and the magnolia scratches
the window. Guerrillas split Beirut,
and Nolan Ryan's worth half a million—
the voice on the tinny Zenith sputters.

Up north trout are game and the Stone Jug's
full of men, and boys who would be men.

for Bruce Smith

Approaching the Summer Solstice

1

Stars have returned to positions
we're familiar with.
It's the kind of night when
only beams beneath the plaster
keep the sky from breaking in.

Today we staked tomatoes.
The runoff from the river
is good fertilizer.

The water gets blacker.
My nose returns without a ripple,
and what's brown besides your eyes
is a home for snakes.

2

You'll wait for birds
or even light
to wrestle my arms loose,
and tell me you've dreamt me
back to water,

scaleless, eel-like
with eyes only large enough
to see shifts in light.

3

Things are screwy.
Too early for cicada.

Tulips gone.
The rose spinning in itself.

4

I want to ask a birch
how it lives in the wind.
I want to ask weeds how
they drink from rocks.

5

On a jetty I can see the eye of a gull.
That's an edge where my arms
and the span of my back
lose their measure.

The sea sends the sun back
through a choroid,
and there's no more current.

The pulse of the heart moves
to the throat,
opens in the jugular.
Rises behind the eyes.

The flat rocks glisten.
Gulls pick-off fish.
My legs feel light as weeds.

★

When the wind comes again
the land is full of flies and dead crabs,
and mussel shells cleaned by the waves.

Algae change color

cormorants are soundless

my ear is hollow

6

The day isn't what you said,
the sun turning the sea to a bed of diamonds,
and the two of us on the sand,
in the grazing foam.

The sun will be overhead soon.
Bring enough vegetables for the long haul.
Greens that can stand the heat.
Rhubarb because it grows in sand,
turnips and potatoes
because they can find water
without light.

7

I'll wake you before
my ears have recovered
from pressure change,

before my eyes have come back
and the salt is dry on my neck,

and I'll swear that a man's scales dissolve
on the ocean floor,

I'll swear that a stream
the width of your foot
is a current.

for Helen

Letting the Fog In

This morning I reach my hand out
the window and slice the air.
I hear the sound of a bird
and lose the sound of my own heart.

I want to hug this air,
and bring it to you,
then let it out slowly
so that it creeps up your toes,
swirls your thin ankle,

then I'd watch it broaden over your thighs,
funnel to your hip and spread the width
of your back. When it rose over the nape
of your neck and your eyes became dim light

I'd assure you that outside fog rises
from puddles, trees are shortened,
and red brick disappears.
Only headlights spoke the air.

I'd promise never to open the window again.
You'd assure me pine needles flicker out there.
Edges of leaves dissolve. Birds cheep far off.

To Hart Crane

This morning kelp dries on the dockside,
women leave the laundromat early.
I walk the bank in the low air
and hear the plumb-sound of the water.

This morning your rib
passes this juncture of ocean and calm.
Here where there's no bridge
and gulls roost on tied barges
and skim the black harbor for carp,
your marrow goes the way of slow mollusks.

The sun moves
in a steady progression upward
to a point—for a fraction of light
before it starts to fall
and here, Hart Crane,
even the falling warehouses
look like cathedrals for a moment.

This morning a drunken fisherman
wakes on cinder with dead bait in his hand,
not knowing the day of week
the month or year—or anything
but the spot he sees the sun in,
the noon wind riveting his ribs.

It's a good thing, Hart Crane,
that I'm baitless and hookless
that I leave the bay without a fish,
my net shredded and hanging on an old post at Fox Point.
It's a good thing my girl took the first train south
and that this noon I unwrap my sandwich alone

under the empty elm with three birds singing in my ears
and the cats meowing over empty clamshells and shrimp husks.

What luck, Hart Crane,
that I came this morning to feel your one bone
dragging along the bottom
just as the sun was climbing to the top
and the fisherman was waking,
just as the tugs were disappearing
and the barges were settling in
to the winter lapping of the harbor,
just as the cod heads were softening around the eye
so the gulls could snap them up.

Robert Lowell Near Stockbridge

The traffic thinned past Chicopee.
Farmland hardened and recalled
Edwards and his relic oak

where a spider set its web
in your heart before you left the Alps.

In the red light of maples
where Edward Taylor once sang
at a wasp pinned in a net

you left your insects for the test
in rotten hollow logs,

and the knot God made in Paradise
tightened on the hills.

Your eye flushed out—
a September morning,
when trees were stitched with webs

too fine to see,
and spiders swam the air
and turned to glisten.

Invisible filaments your heart
gave way before—
a Berkshire hawk dove on them

and left the maples
in their beauty
untenable as gristle.

for Jack Wheatcroft

"My Mother Is a Fish"
—Faulkner

My mother is a fish
and the sky is low and orange,
and the long grass rises
in the still air.
The mud is black
and worms turn
their cold segments
at my feet.

    I used to walk
    with an old lady.
    It seemed far from water
    and the ground sank.
    Weeds were higher
    than my head.
    Slugs slept
    in the mud.

My mother is a fish
and the sky swallows my head.
A fine rain comes
and softens the ferns.

In March before the crocus
and the lily,
eggs bunch in the shoal
of green jelly.
Crabs glide through them.
A kingfisher is dead
on a rock.

My mother is an eel
winding a light

around the rock.
Even without a moon
the black glows.

★

The sun grows like an egg
over the bridge,
the first birds are silver
and swoop down for my mother.

When the lady came
we jumped—
She took us to find worms
we could squeeze
in our hands.

I went with my father
to the dark water.
I went with a bucket
of mud.
When we doubled the worm
on the hook and it coiled,
I could hear how a bass
could thud.

I grabbed it
with a wet hand,
and watched its eye
go black
as I dropped it
in a metal bucket.

*Hack it along the gill
and throw the head to the gulls.*

★

My mother is a fish
and flutters in my bucket.
The sky is a fleck of stones
on the night water.
Turns my arms silver.

The wind calls my father
out to where bigger birds
call and caw and spin,

where my father goes
and leaves me with the mud
and gulls on the patchy water.

Father Fisheye

The sun is gray and without a rim,
what light there is the water catches and keeps.
Fishmongers bear the crossed keys of the saint
on their arms. St Christopher lived on the gulf
and sang for the kingfish when the wind left,
let his arms out from their joints when the old men
left in the dark with their trawl.

Father Fisheye, I come here to the rocks where the fires
are all ash, where the dockmen have disappeared
for the day of Gennaro and the boys with straw hats
have gone with their fathers' empty creels and sandworms
in their pockets, where old men still sit staring
at the short ripples going white at their feet.

I come to this inlet for eels and crabs
for gangs of minnows that move like a long tail
and turn silver in the gray sun.
Father Fisheye, the air is still, trees motionless,
the sky touches my chest.
The sun is lost in the gray dusk water, gone into the gullets
of fishes wandering out to the far waves.

Words for My Grandmother

Rhododendron leaves are hard as wax.
Some chewed-up nests spot my view.
Birds dive behind a flaring neon sign.

I walk in piles of soaked leaves;
a space between stones and trees
of a side lot where you took
shortcuts to the A&P.

Ten years ago I went
once more up narrow steps,
a Karabagh runner worn
like a past half-confessed.

A paper bag of cardamom
on a Wedgwood platter.
Water hissing on the gas flame.
The kitchen fastidious with clatter.

Your hands in fluorescent
kitchen light still discolored
by the arid Turkish crescent.

The Field of Poppies

Cypress spiral to the sky.
Painters came here because the dirt
was dry as bones,
because the monastery on the hill
flaked each day.
I want a picture of you
in this field:
wind blowing the long grass
around your legs,
acres of yellow flowers across
the road moving away from you.
The high mountain is where
the saint disappeared with his wound.
When he returned
apricot trees sprouted from the rock.

Cypress spiral to the sky.
Your father found this field
and the mountain uncovered,
the monastery a glint of sun.
I want this picture
to be your body disappearing
in waves of flower,
a field of pinpricks
rising and falling in the breeze,
each step spreading red.

I want the red to cover the mountain.
I want the line where sky and land meet
to hold like thread.

This is how your father left:
foot, knee, stomach, face
disappearing in the stain,
in light wind, red flowers.

—*for Aunt Gladys and Aunt Alice*

NOTES

"Night Patio": "Saw the heavens fill with commerce, argosies of magic sails," from Tennyson's "Locksley Hall," which Harry Truman carried in his wallet from the age of eighteen and had with him at Potsdam. See *Hiroshima in America: Fifty Years of Denial*, Robert Jay Lifton and Greg Mitchell (Putnam, 1995).

"Harpert, Revisited": Harpert (today renamed Elazig), a historic Armenian city and province of east-central Anatolia in the Ottoman Empire, where the Turkish government slaughtered thousands of Armenians during the Genocide of 1915; Leslie Davis, U.S. consul stationed there, dubbed it "the slaughterhouse province." Excerpts are from Davis's State Department report, *The Slaughterhouse Province: An American Diplomat's Report on the Armenian Genocide, 1915–1917*, ed. Susan K. Blair (Caratzas, 1989). Khatchgar: stone-carved Armenian cross.

"Train to Utica" is indebted to Thomas A. Bass's *Vietnamerica: The War Comes Home* (Soho Press, 1996). *Con lai* is Vietnamese for half-breed.

"Physicians": Adana: province in south-central Turkey where 30,000 Armenians were massacred in April 1909, an event that helped set the stage for the 1915 Genocide. My grandfather worked as a physician aiding the Armenian survivors in Adana in the spring of 1909.

"The Oriental Rug": Kashan: floral Persian rug; madder: herb yielding red dye; genista: spiny shrub yielding yellow dye; Marmara: sea between Asiatic and European Turkey; Adoian: family name of painter Arshile Gorky, who was born in Van; Van: Armenian province in eastern Turkey; Karabagh: mountainous region of Armenia famous for its long rugs.

"Flat Sky of Summer": Kazak: a colorful, bold, geometric rug, indigenous to Armenia and the western Caucasus; Toros Roslin: thirteenth-century Armenian manuscript painter.

"Out of School": Hattie Carol: from Bob Dylan song about an African-American maid who was killed at a society party in Baltimore.

"Last Days Painting (August 1973)": lines in italics are from Vincent van Gogh's letters.

"Camille Claudel, Some Notes": sculptor (1864–1942); was Rodin's collaborator, model, and mistress.

"The History of Armenia": *yavrey,* a Turkish word commonly used among Armenians, meaning dear heart, dearest, etc.

"The Claim": The documentary portions of this poem are from my grandmother Nafina Chilinguirian's (later Aroosian) human rights suit against the Turkish government for losses suffered as a result of the Armenian Genocide. The legal rubric of the document is Claims Against Foreign Governments and was issued by The Department of State, Washington, D.C., May 15, 1919; it was filed by her attorney in Newark, New Jersey, in 1920.

"Seferis Returning to Smyrna, 1950": Greek poet and Nobel laureate George Seferis (1900–1970) was born in the ancient Greek city of Smyrna (today Izmir, Turkey) and fled the city in 1914, when the Turkish government began exterminating and deporting Christians. He returned to his birthplace as a Greek diplomat on assignment in 1950.

ACKNOWLEDGMENTS

Grateful acknowledgment to the magazines in which some of these poems first appeared, sometimes with different titles and in earlier versions.

Agni Review: "In Church," "Lowlands," "To Arshile Gorky," "Physicians," "Morning News"
Antaeus: "Last Days Painting (August 1973)"
Ararat: "Poppies," "In Armenia, 1987," "Words for My Grandmother"
Boulevard: "First Communion"
Carolina Quarterly: "Father Fisheye," "Granny, Making Soup," "Thoreau at Nauset"
Cutbank: "Approaching the Summer Solstice," "A Sequence of Wind Between Seasons"
The Greenfield Review: "Road to Aleppo, 1915"
Illinois Review: "Saigon / New Jersey"
Kenyon Review: "American Dreaming"
New Directions in Prose and Poetry 38: "To Hart Crane," "The Field of Poppies"
New Directions in Prose and Poetry 47: "Night Blue Fishing on Block Island," "Mussel Shell," "Jersey Bait Shack"
The New Republic: "Ellis Island"
Partisan Review: "Mandelstam in Armenia, 1930"
The Phoenix: "Winter Revival"
Ploughshares: "A Letter to Wallace Stevens"
Poetry: "The Oriental Rug," "Fish Mouth," "A Country House," "Flat Sky of Summer," "A Toast," "Domestic Lament"

Poetry East: "After the Survivors Are Gone"
Poetry Northwest: "The History of Armenia," "For My Grandmother,
    Coming Back"
Southern California Poetry Anthology: "Parts of Peonies"
The Southern Review: "Out of School"
Verse: "Jade Boat"
West Branch: "Graham House, April '76"

ABOUT THE AUTHOR

Peter Balakian was born in 1951 and grew up in Teaneck and Tenafly, New Jersey. He holds a B.A. from Bucknell University and a Ph.D. from Brown University. He is the author of four previous books of poems, a translation of the Armenian poet Siamanto, and *Black Dog of Fate,* which won the 1998 PEN/Martha Albrand Prize for the art of the memoir. Between 1976 and 1996, he edited with Bruce Smith the poetry magazine *Graham House Review.* The recipient of numerous prizes and awards, including the Anahit Literary Prize, the New Jersey Council for the Humanities Book Award, and a Guggenheim fellowship, Balakian is the Donald M. and Constance H. Rebar Professor of the Humanities in the department of English at Colgate University. He lives in Hamilton, New York, with his wife, Helen, and their children, Sophia and James.